Putting Down Roots

To Becky

thanks for your
support of the
Arboretum

BOBBI

Endorsements

"I feel we are lucky that Bobbi Lancaster took an interest in volunteering at the Boyce Thompson Arboretum (BTA), an interest that led her to write this charming, yet thought-provoking book that is filled with actual historical information surrounded by some imaginative fiction. Her polished style is the result of many years spent writing her previously published books. Bobbi's lightness of spirit and humor fill the book, even in the sad and the informative portions. And don't be surprised by the sections that involve the reader in deep thought and reflection."

Sylvia Houston Lee, RN
BTA historian and docent

"Bobbi Lancaster lives life with the passion that comes through in her writing. Using the trained eye of a physician, Bobbi gives voice to a proud resident of Arizona's Boyce Thompson Arboretum in order to tell the history of this desert gem. *Putting Down Roots* pulls readers in with raw and honest emotions that deliver a heartfelt recounting of William Boyce Thompson's life and legacy."

A.S. Penne
Author and editor

"I thought that after dozens of visits, I 'knew' Boyce Thompson Arboretum State Park. I didn't. My next visits will be all the richer for what I have learned from Gus and Bobbi's narratives."

Rick Wright
Author, lecturer, tour leader

"*Putting Down Roots* includes an accurate and most evocative description of the dynamic geological history of the Arboretum area; it includes the volcanic eruption of the Superstition Mountains that is recorded in the modern landscape."

Steven Semken, Ph.D, C.I.G.,
Professor of Geology and Education,
School of Earth and Space Exploration,
Arizona State University

Putting Down Roots

Interior Book Design and Layout by
www.integrativeink.com

ISBN: 978-0-578-45246-3

Putting Down Roots

A Story about a Colonel, a Medicine Man and their Garden

Dr. Bobbi Lancaster

WITH A FOREWORD BY

Rick Wright

"History will be kind to me because I intend to write it."

Sir Winston Churchill

"This book is dedicated to the Boyce Thompson Arboretum's staff, volunteers, administrators and board members. Your tireless commitment to the original vision is extraordinary. Every living thing in the garden depends on your care, and they have asked me to express their sincere thanks."

Gus

By the Same Author

The Red Light Runner

Fairway Secrets

My Friend Flutter

Backyard Adventures

TABLE OF CONTENTS

FOREWORD
by Rick Wright

How do you tell the story of a landscape? How do you narrate its geologic past, the nature of its plants and animals, the fates of generations of humans who have lived and died on it? It's too much for even the most ambitious writer to undertake alone.

Bobbi Lancaster had some very special help in her exploration of the lava-rich landscape of what is now Boyce Thompson Arboretum; a venerable saguaro cactus, who his friends call Gus. Gustopher Short Pants is a happy survivor with an incredible memory that almost reaches into the prehistoric past. He punningly describes himself as being "well grounded" in his ecological community. Gus has spent the centuries of his Sonoran desert life storing up not just precious water, but all the stories of the land; carefully gathered over the years from his saguaro ancestors, surrounding plants and animals and even the odd human interlocutor.

As Gus retells the fascinating natural and cultural events to Bobbi, and to us, an elaborate picture emerges of the history of the land around Picket Post Mountain. This very spot witnessed the genocidal depravity of the Indian Wars, the desperation of miners and the dreams of early white settlers. We learn how the land passed from the Apache to the hardscrabble Clevenger family to William Boyce Thompson, whose name it bears today.

Bobbi and Gus tell the Thompson family story in engaging detail, from young Will's peripatetic life on the Montana frontier, to his introduction to genteel New England, followed by his tremendous success as a mine owner and investor. The acquisition of a mine in Superior, Arizona, would change his life forever: William Boyce Thompson fell in love with the rugged landforms and abundant wildlife of the Sonoran Desert. In an inspired piece of poetic justice, he dedicated the wealth he had made by despoiling landscapes to preserving the natural beauty that surrounded the magnificent winter house he would build there.

Thompson was that rarest of people; a genuinely effective dreamer, putting his energy and money into projects ranging from agricultural reform to the spectacular botanical garden we enjoy today. He did not work alone, of course, and in a truly eye-opening story, Gus and Bobbi introduce us to Thompson's right-hand man in the construction of the garden: the brilliant and hard-working Natchilta (Nat Patterson), an Apache who for forty years had the satisfaction of living a simple life on the land taken from his ancestors, half a century before.

Like many readers, I thought that after dozens of visits, I "knew" Boyce Thompson Arboretum State Park. I didn't. The lives of those who have left their mark and their memory on this piece of desert were more complex and complicated than I ever suspected. My next visits will be all the richer for what I have learned from Gus and Bobbi's narratives.

How do you tell the unbelievable story of a landscape? It's all quite simple. Just read on and find out.

Rick Wright, PhD
Author, editor and lecturer
Victor Emanuel Nature Tour Leader

Gus, as a middle-aged cactus

PROLOGUE

My name is Gustopher Short Pants. A long time ago, a group of Indian boys met regularly and played bow and arrow games at the foot of Magma Ridge where I live. Their laughter was contagious, their antics were hilarious and I often found myself chuckling along with them. However, one day their behavior took a dark turn; while walking by, they abruptly stopped and stared. They pointed at my admittedly dirty brown feet and exposed lower leg and started to laugh and tease me; they called me Mr. Short Pants and shot some arrows in my direction. Thankfully they were not good marksmen. Nevertheless, I felt frightened and vulnerable for the first time in my life and I was more than a little humiliated.

You see, the green jumpsuit I was born with was one size too small and the pant leg did not extend down to the ground. To make matters worse, I did not have any shoes. Unfortunately their nickname stuck and everyone started to call me Short Pants in a mocking sort of way. My real friends call me Gus and I have been standing tall and proud for many years in the arboretum, before it was called an arboretum.

Other than a few creosote bushes, I believe I am one of the oldest residents. In fact I'm so old that I can recall the Tonto Apache Indians going about their business of farming and hunting just over the rise. The early years were quite calm and uneventful, almost monotonous. Today feels very much like tomorrow and yesterday, if you get my drift. But somewhere along the way, this beautiful place was turned upside down and now I feel like I have seen just about enough. By the way, did I mention I am a *Carnegiea gigantea*, otherwise known as a saguaro cactus? You heard me correctly: I'm a cactus and I am very well grounded.

Last week at the end of yet another hot and sleepy summer day, Rory, the local rock squirrel, bounded up the lava cliff as though his tail was on fire. He skidded to a dusty stop right in front of me and took a minute to catch his breath. I noticed he was standing on a Harvester ant hole and I urged him to move. As usual he was not listening and within a few seconds was jumping up and down to shake the biting insects from his feet. He looked like a squirrel on a hot tin roof. He excitedly announced there was a new park volunteer called Bobbi and she would like to speak with me. Apparently she heard me crying a couple of days ago and was concerned.

I must admit that for a moment or two, I didn't know what to say. The last human who could hear my voice was an old Indian woman called Two Spirit, and we had many memorable conversations while gazing out at the rhyolite-rich landscape. That was over one hundred years ago. I remember tears streaming down her sad and weathered face as she was carted off to her new home in San Carlos, Arizona. It was a home that she never wanted; a reservation. She called it a prison; others named it "Forty Acres of Hell" because it was basically a barren wasteland. I never saw that wise and quite charming woman again.

It's always puzzled me that people are unable to hear the plant and animal voices all around them, because we are a noisy bunch. There were times when I would scream at the top of my stomata in an effort to grab the attention of a passing human, and they would continue to walk by completely absorbed in their own world. And now quite unexpectedly, someone called Bobbi can hear me and I am thrilled to know we will actually speak soon. I didn't fully realize until this moment how much I had missed talking with humans. I instructed Rory to run back down the hill and arrange the meeting before Bobbi changed her mind. Of course she would have to navigate the steep and slippery climb to meet with me because I do not travel well.

She arrived the next day after a brief but strenuous hike and she was flushed and perspiring heavily. It took several moments for her panting to settle down and then Bobbi introduced herself and proceeded to sit down on that very same ant hill. This was followed by a pants-on-fire moment as she hopped around and frantically slapped at her butt and pant legs. She looked absolutely ridiculous; I laughed so hard that the Gila woodpeckers flew out of my upper arm penthouse suite and asked me to be quiet. I was upsetting their hatchlings. Bobbi finally seated herself on a nearby rock, produced a pad of paper and a pen, and took charge.

I was impressed with her steady gaze and confident demeanor and knew immediately I could trust her. She started the conversation by asking if I was all right, because she had heard me sobbing several days ago. Bobbi informed me that she was writing a book about William Boyce Thompson and a medicine man and the early days of the arboretum; she wanted to learn more from an old-timer like me.

The following pages are a record of our lengthy conversations that transpired over many weeks. Bobbi asked me endless questions and marveled at my memory and my insights. I was curious to know how long she'd been talking to animals and plants. Bobbi stated that as a youngster this ability came naturally to her. For example, she recalled talking to a hummingbird in a neighbor's flower garden and holding out her little hand so the bird could perch confidently on her index finger. The hummer thanked her because it was tired and needed a safe place to rest.

Then quite mysteriously, Bobbi lost the ability to communicate with nature when she grew up and life became more serious. Now that she is much older, Bobbi is ecstatic her special skill has returned; she hopes it will allow her to better tell the arboretum's story.

I have to tell you that during our conversations, staff and visitors would stop and point and snicker at Bobbi while she asked me questions. She seemed oblivious to their disparaging comments. I told her they probably thought she was crazy; Bobbi said she is used to being stared at and made fun of because she is different and their opinions of her really do not matter. Because of my short pants and the teasing I had experienced when I was younger, I could really relate to her and our friendship became even stronger.

Now that I have finished this introduction, it's time for you to find a comfy spot and relax. As you turn to the first chapter, ready yourself, because you are about to be amazed by this old cactus' recollections and storytelling. Enjoy and please be careful you're not sitting on an ant hill.

Gus

"Tears are the silent language of grief."

Voltaire

"There is no grief like the grief that does not speak."

Henry Wadsworth Longfellow

CHAPTER ONE

CRYING AT THE SKY

Yes, I was crying the other day because it was the anniversary of a sad and very personal event. Let me explain. When I was about a hundred years old, I'd produced an extraordinary profusion of flowers on the top of my head and arms. They were stunningly white and fragrant, if I don't say so myself. Hundreds of people stopped to take pictures of me and as an added bonus, my blossoms attracted bees and birds from all over the arboretum. But the most distressing thing occurred at night, because my flowers proved to be irresistible for the Mexican long-tongued bats. They would land on each blossom and stick their tongues deep into the nectar. Their licking and slurping would keep me awake for hours and it tickled intensely. They drove me nuts and I thought I would die of "restless blossom syndrome." I was going out of my mind and now you know where the expression "going batty" comes from.

My pollinated flowers eventually became tantalizing, blood-red fruit and over a dozen doves arrived one morning and stuffed their faces all day. It was embarrassing to watch. Finally satisfied, these feathered gluttons waddled toward the end of my arms and perched, exposing their bloated bellies for all to see. I shivered in an effort to shoo them away; they were too heavy to fly. After what seemed like hours, they pooped out many tiny saguaro seeds right at my feet and then flew off as if drunk. To be honest, I prayed they'd be stopped at the FUI (flying under the influence) checkpoint located in the park, because it would serve them right.

I talked to those little seeds as they organized themselves in front of me and I tried my best to get them to roll down the slope to a sheltered location. Most of them did not listen, including one of them named Hope. After bouncing down the rocky surface, she came to rest agonizingly close to a potential nurse tree. It was at that moment she decided to put down her roots. I knew it would be touch and go, because a young saguaro cannot tolerate constant full sun exposure.

The lifesaving shade provided by a nearby mesquite tree was only several feet away and Hope was just outside its circle of protection. However by some miracle she reached nine years of age and she was beautiful. Hope had an amazing spirit and so many dreams; she was a talker too. I held my breath and dared to believe she would survive.

That tenth summer was brutally hot and the rain never came. Her conversations became abbreviated and I noticed the color leave her face. It was on a dry and windy afternoon when Hope toppled over and her withered little body tumbled down the slope and out of sight. At first I didn't grasp what I had just observed and after several stunned seconds, I exploded from a place deep inside me that I didn't know existed. It ripped me apart and even my skin started to split open. The shock waves created by my wailing pulsed in every direction and my friends suddenly realized what had happened; there was a collective gasp and a moment of silence.

My Inca Dove buddies were particularly grief stricken; several of them started to chant. Within the hour, all of the Incas were repeating their simple but touching refrain: "No Hope…no Hope." Their message of despair spread quickly throughout the entire region and it has been passed along to subsequent generations. It serves as a painful reminder every single day of my loss.

It was on my Hope's day of remembrance that Bobbi heard me crying. To be honest, I really don't want to talk about this sad event anymore except to say that Hope was so full of promise and her passing left me with an emptiness that has never been filled. She was my one and only love.

"Civilization exists by geological consent, subject to change without notice."

Will Durant

CHAPTER TWO

BEGINNINGS

I'm sure you are wondering how I can be such a terrific witness to history when I am fixed in one location. It's actually quite simple when you have as many friends as I do. Aside from Rory, there are the woodpeckers, flickers, cardinals, cowbirds and doves. There are also Harris antelope squirrels, cliff chipmunks, whiptails, earless lizards, dragonflies, Lyre snakes and more. And at night, you would be amazed to see the ring-tailed cats, kit foxes, raccoons, coati, bobcats and even a mountain lion. All of these amigos serve as my eyes and ears and keep me informed.

I almost forgot to include the gossipy Yellow-breasted Chats and the Bell's vireos, whose conversations sound like they are asking repeatedly for directions to Wichita. The migrating birds and Monarch butterflies bring me news from afar as well. And once this place became a park in the 1920s, the visitors proved to be a treasure trove of information. Some of them were former teachers and classmates of William Boyce Thompson; others were old friends and neighbors of his. All I had to do was listen to their conversations swirling around me. In a nutshell, this is how I know so much.

Bobbi had no idea how well connected I was. She was obviously eager to get started and looked anxiously at the many prepared questions scribbled on her notepad. She began by suggesting I talk about the early history of the area. Of course I inquired how far back she wanted me to go and Bobbi suggested I could choose the starting point. Since there were no restrictions, I decided to give her the full treatment and show off.

"About 18 million years ago, a huge volcano complex existed in what is now the Gold Canyon area, about twenty-five miles west of here. It was on a beautiful summer afternoon when extremely hot and sticky rhyolite, located deep below the earth's crust, found its way through a fault to the surface; having been pushed up by incredible pressure from below. The magma exploded outward with the force of a nuclear bomb. A cloud of ash and toxic gas as hot as molten glass was blasted thousands of feet into the atmosphere and melted everything in its path as it drifted east. The ash settled around what's now called the arboretum and the town of Superior; once cooled, this hardened fallout, called tuff, was hundreds of feet deep in places.

"Over the next few million years, the original volcano complex became a giant sink-hole because it had literally disgorged its deeper rhyolite; there was nothing left below to support the ground above. This collapse created a huge depression called a caldera many miles wide. As time passed, deeper rock was pushed up by the continued extreme pressure from below. It was a relatively easy push, so to speak, because the weight of the magma that had once kept these rocks down was long gone. These pushed-up formations are referred to as resurgence and we now call them the Superstition Mountains.

"To complicate things further, a new and smaller volcano formed to the south of my location about 16 million years ago and it's now called Picket Post Mountain. Rhyolite lava flowed out a vent and piled up, like a giant snow drift, at the base of the mountain; we call this area Magma Ridge. Some of the lava rolled downhill and gathered up rocks; they are called block and ash formations. This process is akin to rolling a snow ball down a hill to make a snow man, with leaves getting stuck in the ever-growing ball.

"Next, the earth's crust became stretched and a giant fault developed around the town of Superior. The land south and west dropped down hundreds of feet and became a basin. The arboretum is located in this basin. Eventually Silver King Wash and Queen Creek flowed into this area from the elevated land, called a range, left behind. I'm living at the site of this ancient, cataclysmic event and it boggles the mind."

I paused and looked over at Bobbi; she had stopped writing and her mouth was agape. She appeared stupefied and exclaimed, "Gus, where in the world did you learn about all of this geology stuff? And don't tell me one of your fury little friends told you about it!"

I blushed, so to speak, and then confessed, "I've been eavesdropping on lectures given by an Arizona State University geology professor named Steven Semken. He often brings his students to the arboretum on field trips and he invariably stops right in front of me to answer questions. Steve conducts tours for the public as well and I am able to catch some of their conversations as they walk by. I'm still trying to grasp the theories involving tectonic plates and I have so many questions. Unfortunately Dr. Semken is not able to hear me."

Bobbi told me she was very impressed with my knowledge of this complicated topic. However she gently suggested I limit my remarks to more recent history, perhaps events that have taken place in the last two hundred years. She explained it would be impossible for her to write a book encompassing millions of years and she wanted to focus on the early story of the arboretum.

Actually this was a relief for me because, to be honest, my grasp of prehistoric events is quite shallow. "Please don't tell anyone."

"Only when the last tree has died,
the last river been poisoned
and the last fish been caught,
will we realize we cannot eat money."

Cree Indian proverb

CHAPTER THREE

GREAT DISRUPTION

I took a minute or two to reorganize my thoughts and decided to restart the storytelling around the time of my birth. I told Bobbi that my father had shared interesting memories with me when I was a young cactus and I thought her future readers would find them fascinating too. It would help set the stage on which this beautiful arboretum was built.

Bobbi liked this idea. However she asked me to promise I would not start talking about dinosaurs or the Big Bang Theory, because she didn't have that kind of time. She reminded me that eventually she wanted to ask questions about the garden.

I apologized profusely for showing off and reassured her that this would not happen again. Without further delay, I began by explaining that my father had lived about fifty feet above me and he died quite suddenly after being struck by lightning many years ago. One day he was forty feet tall and full of life and stories. After the storm passed, he was limp and speechless; he literally dissolved from view over the next several years. I have closed my eyes a hundred times and tried to remember the sound of his voice. However, that aural memory has been lost.

Before he was silenced, he regaled everyone with stories. He also chided me constantly about how easy my life was; he was right. To be sure, I was aware that living in the desert was challenging and a drop of water could mean the difference between life and death. However, I had a supportive cactus community surrounding me and lots of pollinator friends. Even the cavity-dwelling birds were careful not to build too many holes in my growing body. Everything was in balance.

My father was not the only source of information. Several turkey vulture friends, when they weren't preoccupied with smelling their way through history, served as important reporters too. They would return home after a long day of soaring brimming with news and roost on the nearby cliffs. I learned a great deal during their debriefings.

On a personal note, when they took off from their overnight perches, they would always poop to lighten their loads, making take-off easier. I was standing in the middle of their runways and they would shower me with excrement; I'd stink and look disgusting until the next cleansing rainstorm. However, I did not complain because their information was invaluable.

When I was about five years old, my dad told me about the Tonto and Yavapai Apache Indians who also called the area home. Their roots were as deep and intertwined as ours and they interacted with nature in a very gentle and respectful manner. They were continuing in the tradition of their ancestors, the Salado people, who had lived in the area hundreds if not thousands of years before. The Apache, the plants and the animals were all one; everyone knew their place and it was all quite simple. Then the troubles started.

Spanish-speaking strangers from a place to the south called Mexico slowly appeared in the early 1800s and claimed the land surrounding my father. At about the same time, English-speaking settlers were moving in from the north and the east, and they were staking claims of their own. The Indian community was caught in the middle. They tried, for the most part, to stay out of the way as the tensions mounted between the Mexicans and the Americans.

At about that same time a young Chiricahua Apache boy was born in what is now called Clifton, Arizona. He was not a Yavapai or Tonto Apache like the natives around where I stand. He was from the southeast part of the territory, almost in Mexico; his story is very important. This babies name was Goyaale, which when translated means "the one who yawns" and we were both born on June 16, 1829. Neither one of us were issued birth certificates.

He grew to be a handsome and strong young man and participated with his elders on overnight trips to trade with the outsiders. The Spanish-speakers were particularly intrigued by the bright red color of some of the Apache's clothes. The Indians taught them that the red dye was obtained by crushing the female cochineal beetles that excreted a white, sticky paste while they fed on prickly pear plants dotting the area. Upon hearing this, you would have thought the strangers had just been told where gold could be found. Make no mistake: they really were looking for gold. However, they instantly recognized the amount of money to be made by selling this cochineal dye in Europe. There were prickly pear cactus back in their ancestral home; all that was missing was the beetles.

Goyaale observed that the Americans and the Mexicans did not have a good grasp of how nature and the Indians had compromised over a long period of time. And both seemed intent on acquiring more land and imposing their religion, culture, rule of law and agriculture on an area that was unprepared and ill-suited. They were also obsessed with striking it rich. The most disturbing thing was how outnumbered the Indians were and the reality that the outsiders had extremely powerful weapons. The only thing in the Indian's favor was the fact that the intruders were more interested in fighting each other, and my goodness, did they ever fight.

It was during the ugly and bloody Mexican-American War that Goyaale was finally welcomed into manhood by his elders. He became known as Geronimo and married a woman called Alope. He was now one of the protectors of the tribe and a defender of their historical sacred land. He accepted the challenge while the war raged on around them. Of course he and others tried to make nice as they continued trading with the Mexicans and the Americans. However, it was inevitable his people would become involved in the bigger conflict.

Thankfully, in 1848, peace was declared and the conflict between the Mexicans and Americans ended. Mexico ceded what is now northern Arizona to the United States and the southern part of this new territory was acquired with the signing of the Gadsen purchase in 1853.

I noticed out of the corner of my eye that Bobbi was shifting positions and I asked her very directly, "Am I boring you to death with my recollections?"

Bobbi looked at me with a surprised expression and said, "Heck no. I was just reaching for a fresh pen. I have never heard history told in this way and your story-telling has completely captivated me. Please keep going."

That was all I needed to hear because, quite frankly, I was just getting warmed up. The next few pages are going to expose what happens when human behavior is left unchecked. The depravity and cruelty can be astonishing.

"In 1858, Geronimo led a small group on yet another trading mission into northern Mexico. When he returned home, he discovered to his horror that their small encampment had been raided by an estimated 400 Mexican troops, under the leadership of Colonel Carrasco. Apparently they had blamed Geronimo for some earlier transgression and decided to attack in a cowardly manner while the men were away. Geronimo's wife, their three children, his mother and several guards were brutally murdered and their horses and supplies were seized.

"Geronimo assessed the carnage and his heart turned to stone. In that terrible moment of grief, he dedicated the rest of his life to resistance and revenge. Cochise and other young Apache men experienced similar events and now the Indian wars in this area had begun. These warriors defended the only home they had ever known with all their might. Motivated by opportunity, retaliation and hate, they raided Mexican and American villages alike. Many murders were committed on both sides during this deadly game of tit for tat and it was a time of lawlessness and savagery. I'll return to the Geronimo story in a few minutes: first, I'd like to talk about the Indian resistance right here at my feet.

"The local Apaches communities were being pushed off traditional land they had farmed for years and used for hunting, just like the Chiricahua. Many new settlers were brazen in their efforts to cleanse the area of the natives; they shot them for sport and collected scalps to redeem them for payment from the military. One day in the Superstition Mountain wilderness, a rancher named Woolsey organized an ambush and slaughtered many Apache; the event has been referred to as the Bloody Tanks Massacre.

"The United States government finally got involved and sent the cavalry, led by General Crook and others, to subdue the natives and establish peace. Military camps named Fort McDowell, Fort Reno, Fort Apache, Camp Verde and many more were organized throughout the region.

"Even in our own backyard, we had military presence. A General Stoneman established a camp and posted troops at the base of Picket Post Mountain, not far from where I am standing. I remember hearing him bark orders as he sent a picket of soldiers, with a large portable mirror, to the top of the mountain. Now you can appreciate how the mountain got its name.

"Once they arrived at the summit, the soldiers had a panoramic view of the surrounding area and they could observe the movements of the Indian warriors. They sent heliographic signals using Morse code to various lookouts around the countryside and troops were dispatched to intercept and do battle with the natives.

"Under the leadership of Chief Delshay, the Apache proved to be fierce warriors. However, their primitive weapons were no match against the guns and overwhelming manpower of the cavalry. The skirmishes were more like executions. Many sites of these Indian massacres are memorialized, including Bloody Basin, Cibecue and Camp Grant. One of the most gruesome incidents occurred when the cavalry cornered several dozen Apache men, women and children on a rock wall above the Salt River; they shot them all and left their bodies unburied. Their skeletons could be seen for years to come and served as a warning to other tribes. It became known as the Skeleton Cave Massacre.

"It wasn't just the cavalry who were pursuing the Indians. Several militia groups made up of regular armed citizens and recruits from other Indian tribes were hunting the Apache as well. As exemplified by this next story, these groups were just as ruthless.

"Approximately seventy-five Apache warriors on horseback were cornered on a cliff above Superior by one of these large citizen militias. Rather than be captured, the Indians galloped or jumped off the precipice to their deaths. This site became known as Apache Leap. There are white perlite rocks with black obsidian inclusions found in the area and they're called Apache Tears. These geological oddities remind us of the grotesque, inhumane moments that have occurred in this otherwise rugged but beautiful landscape.

"By 1873, Chief Delshay had witnessed enough suffering and brutality and he surrendered. The remaining Apache were rounded up and moved to a newly created internment enclosure near Camp

Verde, in the center of the territory. There was no room to hunt and gather or practice their customary way of life; malaria and small pox broke out, starvation occurred, and death was everywhere. Out of desperation, many Apache attempted escape. This reservation site was clearly not working and a new location called San Carlos, to the southeast, was prepared.

"The year was 1875 and in a gesture of extraordinary cruelty, the military decided to march the remaining Apaches one hundred and fifty miles over wild and rugged wilderness in a direct line from Camp Verde to San Carlos. The cavalry, who were on horseback, could have directed their captives along pre-existing, more level trails. However, it appears they wanted to torture the natives; during this forced march now called The Exodus, one hundred Indians died.

"The conditions at the new reservation quickly became just as deplorable as the previous internment camp. This was where my friend, Two Spirit, had been sent; I shudder to think what probably happened to her.

"And guess who else ended up in San Carlos? It was Geronimo and other members of his Chiricahua tribe, and he was not in the mood to accept the intolerable situation for even one more minute.

"I was born where there were no enclosures,"
Geronimo

"You might as well expect rivers to run backwards as any man born free to be contented penned up."
Chief Joseph

"He revolted and escaped with his band of loyal warriors to the familiarity of the Sierra Madre in Sonora, Mexico. From there they continued their resistance, raids and disruption; they proved to be a major impediment toward the establishment of law, order and peaceful living in the southwest.

"At some point the federal government's patience was exhausted and in1882, General Crook was instructed to find and remove this last resistor named Geronimo. This was the same General Crook who had been ordered to end the Sioux Indian Wars in Montana six years earlier. The Sioux had defeated and killed General Custer at the Battle of the Little Big Horn in 1876. Under the direction of Generals Crook, Terry and Miles, the Seventh Cavalry successfully captured the Sioux Indian leaders, including Crazy Horse. The Sioux had tried to hold on to their land, sacred places and way of life too. In the end they were absolutely crushed by the military.

"General Crook now turned his attention to the last pocket of native resistance in the country. He knew what he was doing and this character called Geronimo would pose no problem for him at all. However, it took him two years of playing cat and mouse with the Apache leader and several dozen of his warriors until they were captured in the mountains of northern Mexico. General Crook triumphantly, but carefully, transported his captives back to Arizona. Apparently Geronimo feared he would be executed as they approached the territorial border; he hatched a daring plan and escaped unharmed with his warriors to northern Mexico again. I'm certain this proved very embarrassing for the General.

"Having been humiliated, General Crook mounted a new campaign to recapture Geronimo. This time he assembled an overwhelming military force comprised of five thousand soldiers and five hundred Indian scouts who'd become part of an auxiliary division. Some of these scouts were Apache who had become enamored with Crook's overall fairness and wanted to help him put an end to the conflict. In 1886 they marched into the Sierra Madre to capture Geronimo, dead or alive.

"I heard an interesting story about General Crook's campaign a month ago, as told by Rick

Wright. Rick is an internationally known bird expert and an acclaimed nature guide. He was visiting the arboretum and presented several lectures and conducted bird walks; during one of his walks, he stopped within earshot and spoke about Crook. Apparently the General was an avid birder, and while he waited for his scouts to find Geronimo, he passed the time and went birding.

"Back in the 1800's, going birding meant you shot the bird you were observing so you could identify and examine it in great detail. Apparently he was focusing on what he thought were two Broad-billed Hummingbirds; he shot both for closer inspection. The Apache warriors hiding nearby heard the shots, located the General and captured him! I'm not kidding. You cannot make this stuff up.

"Geronimo was stunned by this unexpected turn of events; he thought he now possessed a very important hostage who could be used as leverage during future negotiations. However, he quickly realized how overwhelmed he and his warriors were by the sheer number of American soldiers converging on the area. Geronimo was also confused and saddened to see how many members of his own Apache tribe had joined forces with the military to secure his capture.

"He surrendered again. Famous photos of him were taken by the legendary C.S. Fly, a famous southwest photographer, who documented many historical events in a very characteristic style.

Geronimo, 1886

(Public domain)

"Geronimo was once again under extremely heavy guard as the long march back to the Arizona territory commenced. This time there would be no missteps. But as the entourage approached Fort Bowie, Geronimo miraculously escaped again!

This was beyond belief and it further enhanced his reputation for having preternatural deception and survival skills. It also proved to be the final embarrassment for General Crook.

"After this debacle, it came as no surprise when Crook was replaced by Brigadier General Miles. With the help of the cavalry and an Apache-speaking West Point graduate named Lieutenant Charles Gatewood, Geronimo was quickly located and surrendered for the third and final time in 1887.

"Once I moved about like the wind.
Now I surrender to you and that is all."
Geronimo

"He was declared a prisoner of war and was transferred, along with other captive warriors, to Fort Pickens in Pensacola, Florida. Obviously the authorities wanted him as far away as possible from his Arizona home.

"While Geronimo was in custody, the public clamored to see this larger than life character. Hundreds were allowed entry to the military jail where they could walk by his cell and view him. He became a celebrity, somewhat akin to the so-called freaks on display at a circus. As for the other

Apache Indians who were imprisoned at Fort Pickens, many died of tuberculosis.

"Back in Arizona, further measures were taken to ensure this tribe would be weakened beyond recovery. Hundreds of Apache children were separated from their families and sent to faraway locations for education and assimilation into mainstream white society. At places like the Carlisle Indian Industrial School in Pennsylvania, one third of these children contracted tuberculosis and perished.

"In 1888, Geronimo was transferred to the Mount Vernon Barracks in Alabama along with other tribal members and tuberculosis once again claimed many lives. He was later transferred to Fort Sill in Oklahoma where, despite his imprisonment, he was allowed to cultivate a small plot of land at the periphery of the base. Geronimo also continued to enjoy celebrity status; he was permitted to pose for photos and earn money for this activity. He was a major draw at the St. Louis World Fair in 1904. He was also invited, while under guard, to ride a horse down Pennsylvania Avenue as part of President Teddy Roosevelt's inauguration parade in 1905. Geronimo was dressed as the proud Apache warrior he had once been and was a crowd favorite. In spite of this, President Roosevelt refused to revoke his prisoner of war designation and he was never allowed to return to Arizona.

"Geronimo ultimately died of pneumonia on February 17, 1909 and was buried at the Fort Sill military base cemetery."

At this point, Bobbi interjected and said, "Gus, you have told the story about the defeat of the Apache at the hands of the English-speaking settlers. At times you have interjected some nervous humor. How do you personally feel about this period in the great American story? Were you ever fearful for your own safety?"

"Bobbi, I know I am just a cactus, and in many ways I feel like I am absolutely the wrong individual to talk about these horrors. People will not take me seriously. Having said that, of course I was scared during this chaotic moment in history, and it wasn't just me. All of my plant and animal friends feared for their lives too; in many ways we were even more vulnerable than the Indians. We didn't have identification documents either, even though we and our ancestors had lived here for thousands of years; there was nothing we could do if someone really wanted to kick us off our land. We were defenseless and could be bulldozed into oblivion tomorrow if developers wanted to satisfy their greed and ambition, in the name of progress.

"Can you imagine what would happen to me if someone wanted my spot on Magma Ridge, ripped me from my roots, and planted me in Pennsylvania or Florida? I have not evolved to survive in places like that. I would almost certainly die and that is exactly what happened to the Apache when they were moved too far from their natural home.

"Bobbi, this period in American history disgusts me. There was no attempt made to embrace others and celebrate diversity. Talking about it is really upsetting and I think it is best I stop and change the subject. There is nothing more ridiculous than seeing a saguaro with short pants, standing on a soap box, ranting about injustice.

"However, at least the reader has a better understanding of the events that took place to create the stage on which this beautiful garden was built."

"You have weighed the stars in the balance, and grasped the skies in a span. Take if you must have answer, the word of a common man."

G.K. Chesterton

"God must love the common man, he made so many of them."

Abraham Lincoln

CHAPTER FOUR

THE EVERYMAN

Chatty Cathy was the first to try to break the news. She flew over Magma Ridge one sunny afternoon in 1913 and landed on a thorny, leafless ocotillo branch to my right. The long, slender perch swayed back and forth and made me dizzy as I tried to focus on her bobbing face. I could see she was bursting to share some gossip with me. "Have you heard the laughter yet? Have you seen the new strangers?" I had no idea what she was talking about.

Cathy was the youngest daughter of the Yellow-breasted Chat family that lived in a cottonwood on Queen Creek. She would often fly by to tell me about the happenings on the south side of the ridge. She was just about to answer her own question when Mr. and Mrs. Canyon Wren swooped down from their high and rocky perch. Their distinctive call is hauntingly beautiful, but it's not very uplifting. It is a series of single notes that descend a musical scale and end in a final, somber statement. However it was sufficient to distract Cathy and then the couple blurted out the news: "Gus, the Clevengers have just arrived and they're constructing a shelter as we speak. The best thing of all is they have four kids who are laughing and playing games. They all look so happy. Gus, isn't this wonderful news?"

You should have seen the look on Cathy's face. She had wanted to be the first to tell me, and her scowl would have stopped a sun dial. In any event, this was welcome news because there is nothing better than having young children in the neighborhood.

Before the Clevengers appeared, things had been pretty quiet for at least fifteen years on Magma Ridge. The fun-loving Indian youngsters and their families were long gone and the cavalry had moved on. At times I could hear loud booming sounds from the direction of Apache Leap and my turkey vulture buddies told me the noise was being made by thousands of people gathered around several mining businesses. While the land was laid bare, the smell and dust were unbearable; I noticed an influx of feathered and furry refugees in our neighborhood, seeking a new life in an effort to escape the mess. From time to time, there were bearded men who would set up camp nearby and stay for several months. I never quite knew what they were up to and held my breath; I hoped they were not looking for gold or silver. Thankfully they did not stay long and went on their way.

However, it now appeared we had a real human family making a home in our midst. I became preoccupied with where they had come from and why they were here. I stood in place, as is my routine, and waited for reports from my friends.

Suddenly I realized I'd been blabbering on and had missed the fact that Bobbi wasn't sitting beside me anymore. I gazed down the rocky slope and saw her trudging toward me. I yelled, "Where the heck have you been? I've been talking to myself and I had no idea you were gone. I must have looked like an idiot and now I have to go over everything again. You should have told me you were leaving."

"Gus, would you just calm down," Bobbi said. "I had to go to the restroom and stock up on bottled water too. I told you where I was going, but you were lost in your thoughts. The other thing you have to realize is that I can 'hear' you from afar. We communicate even when I am in the bathroom or while I'm driving home at the end of the day. If you haven't noticed by now, Einstein, you don't have a mouth and a voice box to make noise with. We communicate in a metaphysical kind of way and it doesn't involve sound waves. I've heard everything you've said for the past thirty minutes while I was gone; you don't have to repeat your story."

I was just about to make a sarcastic comment in response when I realized that Bobbi was right. I was irritable because we'd spent every waking minute with each other for too many days in a row. "I'm feeling rather prickly," I said. "How about you Bobbi, are you all right?"

"Actually I'm fine, but I'll let you decide if you want to continue."

After taking a cleansing breath, I shook off the tension of the moment and continued my story. The first bits of research concerning the Clevengers trickled in. The husband's name was Robert and he was born in 1869. His wife's name was Mae and she cared for the four children from his first marriage. Robert's first wife was no longer in the picture because she had struggled with alcoholism and left him with the kids: she had to battle her demons alone. The names of the children were Lucille Elizabeth, Mary Mae, Andrew and William Robert.

It appeared that Robert's plan was to support his family in the brand new state of Arizona by growing and selling fruits and vegetables for the nearby mining camp workers. He chose some land along Queen Creek on the other side of the ridge from me. It was 'owned' by some Mexicans who had never properly registered the property. After money exchanged hands in September of 1913, Robert applied for a title using the new homestead laws. He did not waste any time and while his purchase was being recorded, he built a two-room house, one side of which was the rock wall of Magma Ridge. It included a fireplace in the kitchen and eating area; one bedroom; a slanted tin roof and a dirt floor. The walls were made of fieldstone. Of course there was no electricity or running water and goodness knows where the bathroom was. It was the sort of primitive structure that would have fit right into a neighborhood thousands of years before recorded time.

Clevenger House, circa 1925
(BTA archives)

Robert was obviously very industrious and creative. About fifteen hundred feet upstream from the house, he built a primitive dam in the dry creek bed and ran a pipe downhill to irrigate his soon-to-be-planted garden. The fall and winter rains came and his vegetables and fruit trees flourished. He acquired a horse and a wagon and delivered his produce to the hungry mouths of the miners and their families. According to my sources, his children helped cultivate and weed the garden. They really enjoyed riding in the wagon along with their father as he made his rounds; they sang songs and involved themselves in random mischief too.

I never did see the family because they kept to the creek and there was no road on my side of the ridge. However, this did not stop me from wondering what would possess a man with an uncertain future to move to an unknown place with four children and a new wife in tow. Was he crazy? Was he escaping from a messy past? Was he desperate? Or was he simply a risk-taker who had become part of the stampede of dreamers, all seeking riches and a fresh start in the West?

His wife intrigued me too. I wanted to know if Mae had ever married before and if she had children of her own. What was it about Robert that caused her to fall in love with the man? Did the children respect her, or did they only obey their father? Where did Mae buy clothes and food for the family? How did they stay clean and what did she do to manage their inevitable illnesses and injuries? Did any of them know how to read or write and what was done about the children's education? I wondered if they believed in a God or attended church.

My list of questions was endless and not one of my friends was able to provide any answers. Rory did tell me the Clevengers decorated their house that first Christmas and it looked very pretty; this little tidbit of information gave me cactus bumps. At times I would see a column of smoke rising from the south side of the ridge and I knew it was coming from their chimney. It would drift in my direction and the smell of burning mesquite was intoxicating.

By the way, I asked my mesquite friends how they felt about becoming firewood late in their life. They told me they were proud to be known as the "Tree of Life" and happy to be of use even in death. It was reassuring to learn they didn't have sensory nerves; they felt no pain when they were being cut into pieces.

By all appearances, everything was going well because Robert purchased an adjacent property in 1914; this brought his total acreage to thirty-five. I recently overhead an historian tell her tour group that Mr. Clevenger dug a proper well east of his house around 1920 and it proved to be a much more reliable source of water for the family and his crops. There was also a new state road constructed in 1922, connecting the big city in the west called Mesa with the mining town in the east called Superior. Much later the road would be renamed US 60 and it ran just to the north of my ridge. I could hear cars and trucks travelling up and down the roadway and I wondered if Robert had purchased a truck too. This would have made it a lot easier for Robert to transport his vegetables to his customers.

And then in March of 1923 the laughter suddenly stopped; the Clevengers had disappeared and none of my contacts knew what had happened. "Bobbi, as a new volunteer to the arboretum, can you help me out a little? Have you learned what became of this family?"

"Gus, I think I'll be able to fill in a few gaps for you. I have read several historical documents suggesting that, in spite of appearances, things were not going well financially for the Clevengers. They had tried to sell some of their Queen Creek property in 1917 and 1918, and what had appeared to be a sure sale fell apart when the buyers failed to deliver any money at closing. With much relief, they eventually obtained a line of credit from a local bank and this helped keep food on their table.

"In March of 1923, Robert sold his entire property to Magma Mining Company; Gus, I hope you'll have more to say about this as your storytelling unfolds. He used the money to build a duplex in Superior and he moved his family into one half of the house; he rented the other half. By all reports, Robert looked like an old man even though he was just fifty-four years old: he was physically spent. This was not surprising given how hard he'd worked. He died in 1939, at seventy years of age, and was buried in the Superior cemetery. Reverend Lindbeck, a Seventh Day Adventist preacher from Phoenix, conducted the services and Robert's wife and two daughters attended. At the time of his death, three of his children lived in New York State and his son, William, lived in Pennsylvania. Two of his favorite hymns were sung at his funeral and they were, '*In the Beautiful Land*' and '*Beautiful Isle of Somewhere*'. I hope this information helps you out, Gus."

"Thanks Bobbi. Without your help, I would never have been able to learn why they left so abruptly. Given the choice of hymns at his wake, it appears he was a dreamer and longed for something better. Now I have many more questions for

Robert, but that opportunity has long since passed. I wonder how he would have summed up his life as he approached the end. Or perhaps there never was time for self-reflection because he was always too busy scratching and clawing in order to provide and survive.

"I think that many people, perhaps even Mr. Clevenger, were simply born to situations where they never caught a break. It's kind of like my daughter, Hope: she and others were never lucky enough to enjoy the protection of a 'nurse tree' when they were young. Their fate was sealed almost from the start; thank goodness they were not aware of the futility of their efforts. Nevertheless, Robert's everyman story is important and I hope his descendants will read your book and be enlightened."

"That's pretty deep stuff, Gus. You sure are a thinker. By the way, I almost forgot to tell you that the arboretum historian, Sylvia Lee, recently asked me to accompany her to Superior in order to photograph the Clevenger duplex on North Magma Avenue. She wanted to obtain more current photos than the ones taken over ten years ago when she last visited the site. We walked up and down the street and the house had simply vanished. There were rumors that it had either burned down at the hands of a local arsonist or had been torn down.

In any event, there was not even a splinter of wood left behind."

"While you were describing your adventure with Sylvia, my thoughts flashed to my father. After he was struck by lightning and died, his body disintegrated and within several years, there was not a trace of him to be found either; he vanished just like the Clevenger duplex. It's that way for most of us, isn't it?

"When we are alive, we think our existence and accomplishments are of great importance and people will remember us forever and ever. However, after death and in just a couple of generations, we are completely forgotten. Robert's humble stone house on Queen Creek is the exception to that rule, but even it will become dust in time too. I have come to the conclusion that if a legacy is really important to an individual, there is nothing more powerful and long lasting than the written word.

"Please accept my apology, Bobbi. I think I've veered off course and my philosophical comments are slowing us down. After all, it's the history of the place you're after and not some mumblings from an old saguaro. Isn't that right?"

"Give yourself a break, Gus. You've been talking about a lot of emotional events and perhaps this exercise is unlocking upsetting memories. We can stop right now, if you want."

"Oh, I'm all right. Give me a moment to collect my thoughts and let's push on. We're just getting to the really good parts."

CHAPTER FIVE

TOMCAT

In 1923, Robert Clevenger sold his Queen Creek property and the stone house he built, with his own hands, to the Magma Mining Company. Of course companies are owned by people, and it's about time to introduce you to the owner of Magma.

His name was William Boyce Thompson. Both Robert and William were born in 1869, but the trajectory of their lives went in opposite directions. At the time of the sale, Robert was physically spent and almost broke. William was at the top of his game; he had amassed great wealth and was making his dreams come true. There is so much more known about this American success story.

Will, as he was called when he was a youngster, was born at home on May 13, 1869, in the tiny community of Alder Gulch; it is now called Virginia City, Montana. The Gold Rush hysteria was on full display and the local mine was the focus of everyone's attention. The doctor who'd delivered young Will had his own story to tell. His wife and children had been killed by Sioux Indians while they were on their way to join him. Outwardly he would have been admired for his knowledge and kindness, but inside his heart was cold and full of revenge.

Baby Will's father was called William, too. Originally from Canada, he quit school at eleven, piloted boats on the Great Lakes for work at sixteen and became a carpenter two years later. In 1865, he developed a case of gold fever, loaded his tools and headed for California. His wagon was being pulled by oxen and he was towing two more wagons and a cow behind. Later he told his family of skirmishes with Indians along the way, so he'd changed plans and diverted to Montana. He arrived in Alder Gulch with only one wagon and the cow which had taken the place of an ox. William established the first sawmill in the region and provided lumber for home construction and the mine in nearby Virginia City.

William Thompson Sr. as an older man

(Courtesy of Boyce Thompson)

While getting started, he met a young lady by the name of Anne Boyce who'd come from a southern plantation and slave-owning family. Her father had escaped the horrors of the civil war and moved his loved ones to a new life out west. As luck would have it, Anne met William and they were married a short time later.

Anne was a quiet, sensitive person and experienced difficulty adjusting to life in this chaotic, noisy, smoke-belching mistake of a place. Anne became a mother and homemaker; she had a total of ten children of whom Will was the first. Only five of her children would actually reach adulthood.

Anne Thompson
(Courtesy of Boyce Thompson)

Like everyone else in a hardscrabble place like Alder Gulch, young Will had to grow up fast and be sturdy too. By the age of five, he was given his own horse and was responsible for its grooming and well-being. He was often seen on horseback earning money for the family by herding the neighbor's cows. He loved being in the country where it was quiet and he was free; he would explore, collect minerals and enjoy nature. Back in town, he was part of a gang of young boys who constantly had mischief on their minds. His nickname was Tomcat and he was one of the main pranksters; he frequently pestered his parents for any kind of a pet, especially a dog, but his stern father wanted nothing to do with animals.

Fear often gripped the community because the Indian wars were swirling around town. Everyone in Montana had heard about the recent Sioux victory over General Custer not that far away; Will's father always armed himself when making lumber deliveries.

By the age of ten, Will's family had moved to the town of Sheridan and then to Glendale to be near the newest can't miss mine where they set up yet another saw mill. Tomcat was still herding cows when he started a new venture: he collected tin cans, melted them in a fire pit and retrieved the lead solder used to weld the seams. He sold it for a handsome profit.

The mine dried up rather quickly in Glendale and the family was on their way to Butte, Montana: a rowdy, sometimes lawless place where the gold-crazed masses rushed next. Butte by comparison made Alder Gulch look serene. However, just as the mine was failing, silver and finally copper were discovered. The elder William eventually constructed thirteen saw mills and business was booming.

The entire landscape around Butte was treeless and ugly; open roasting ovens and smelters constantly belched sulfur-smelling smoke. Miners were entertained by women, whisky, dice and brawls. Will noticed that his mother appeared sickly, mournful and out-of-place. He tried to cheer her up by planting flower gardens around their house; the choking fallout from the smoke stacks landed on the plants and killed them all very quickly. This was not a place for flowers or delicate souls.

The mining business and the surrounding neighborhoods had a voracious appetite for wood and the Thompson family was very happy to fill this need. Tomcat's father was doing quite well financially and became popular; at one point he even became mayor of this unruly place.

Will was now well into his teens and delivering wood by wagon for the family business and handling payments too. He was also spending time in the saloons where he learned to play cards. He quickly mastered numbers and probabilities and excelled at poker; his pockets were often bulging with cash at the end of the day.

Tomcat, kneeling at the bottom of the photo (BTA archives)

"Bobbi, can you believe how much I've learned over the years from arboretum docents walking by with park visitors in tow? The stories are so interesting. Have you noticed I haven't mentioned anything up to this point about Will attending school?"

"Of course I've noticed. His childhood was certainly like nothing I am familiar with. Did he ever go to school, or was it assumed he was going to follow in his father's footsteps and a formal education was unnecessary?"

"Well he did attend classes sporadically as a youngster. However, after a series of unexpected events, he finally started school full-time when he was about fifteen. Let me explain.

"A wealthy mine engineer in Butte had hired a tutor from England to live with his family and teach his children. The engineer was caught stealing money and he and the family had to get out of town at midnight. That left the tutor, Arthur Cotton Newell, with no work or place to live. He was quickly installed as the principal of the newly created Butte General School and Will was enrolled.

"Many men in the town were opposed to formal teaching, especially by an Englishman; their children picked up on those attitudes and became unruly. It was a very rocky start for this new teacher. However, little by little, Mr. Newell won over Will Thompson. He introduced him to the bigger world and surreptitiously sent him adventure books. He recognized Will's ability with mathematics and his love of beauty, nature and science. He was also concerned that his young student had difficulty expressing himself and appeared undisciplined.

"At about this same time, Will's mother had become weaker and was spending winters in California. She had been diagnosed with a kidney ailment called Brights Disease along with what some have described as her whining, neurotic personality. Without her in Butte all the time, Will felt less inclined to stay; he was a restless seventeen years of age and wanted more than Butte could offer.

"I'd love to have been a cactus on the wall when Will discussed going away to school with his parents. He waited until his mother was present to have this difficult conversation, because old man Thompson was known to be abrupt. There were stories about how he scared the children to death with his high-pitched voice, religiosity and hypercritical commentary. He was openly disappointed in his underperforming oldest child and readily agreed to send Will off where he might finally make something of himself. Almost too eagerly, he agreed to pay for a boarding school anywhere and left the selection to his son.

"Will decided to go to Phillips Exeter Academy in New Hampshire, because the famous Daniel Webster had gone there. He was not related to the Webster of dictionary fame; I wonder if Will was aware of that fact.

"He packed his clothes, donned a derby cap and the full length frock-coat his father had purchased for him, grabbed his playing cards and finally arrived in Exeter on January 1, 1887.

"A man's worth is no greater than his ambitions."

Marcus Aurelius

"Talented people hit targets no one else can hit.
Ambitious people aim to hit targets
no one else can see."

Addoo S. Mukhtar

CHAPTER SIX

GO EAST YOUNG MAN

"How do you think young Will Thompson was received on his first day at Exeter, Bobbi? Remember he was arriving from the frontier and was trying to blend in to life in a more refined New England."

"My guess is it would have been a rough welcome, Gus."

"Rough is putting it mildly. They mocked his clothes. They made fun of his pompadour hair style. Even the mathematics teacher suggested he should go back to live with his half-breed friends in Montana.

"But everything changed after the first week when several classmates invited Will to join them in a card game. He dazzled them with his poker skills; this created instant notoriety for Will and he fit in quite nicely after all.

"The school offered many scholarships, so the poor and wealthy rubbed shoulders together. There was no division by social class. The education style and curriculum were very liberal and democratic; the process involved seating the students at circular tables which encouraged engagement and discussion. Athletic prowess was revered and in that department, Will was sadly lacking.

"Some modern day graduates of Exeter include Mark Zuckerberg; authors Gore Vidal and Dan Brown (*Da Vinci Code*); a hedge fund wizard called Tom Steyer and a filmmaker named John Irving (*Cider House Rules, World According to Garp*).

"Thompson was not an outstanding student. When he returned home to visit his family in Butte during the first summer break, his father discovered Will sleeping with gloves on and demanded an explanation. Will told him he put cream on his hands every night to soften them and that he wore gloves to keep the cream from wiping off on the bed sheets; people were making fun of his calloused hands back at Exeter. Apparently his father went ballistic and expressed more disappointment in Will.

"He returned to Exeter and continued his studies. Will developed his social skills by attending dances; he enjoyed the theater and became friends with several young ladies at the nearby all-girls school.

"A seminal moment occurred in Will's young life during a school break, when he travelled to New York City and visited the New York Stock Exchange. From the visitors' gallery, he watched the traders in the pit below, waving and shouting frantically as they bought and sold mining stocks. Will knew the mines intimately and could tell the traders were promoting mines that were next to useless. Not only that, he was mesmerized by the numbers and risk-taking because it reminded him of playing poker, except on a grander scale. It was at that moment his future became crystal clear: he was going to own and invest in mines and make a fortune on the New York Stock Exchange.

"Another life-changing event happened at Exeter that involved religion. Will's family members were devout Methodists, but he did not believe in all the miracles and the Christ story. He had also witnessed the discrimination and prejudice between Irish Catholics and the Protestants in Butte while growing up, and this furthered his doubts about the value of organized religion. However, he'd never felt at liberty in Montana to discuss these feelings, especially with his pious father. At Exeter, there was ample opportunity for him to question and debate; in the end, he emerged as a skeptic, considered himself a non-believer and felt no shame in adopting this position.

"After three years at Exeter, Will had enough credits to qualify for the Columbia School of Mines in New York City. He was accepted and completed one year of study. I remember hearing a docent at the arboretum read his report card to a tour group: Chemistry 46; Chemical analysis 52; Geometry 62; Algebra 79; and Botany 81. When three years at Exeter and one year at Columbia were added together, Will was finally able to matriculate from high school.

"He returned to Butte for the summer break in 1890 to discover his beloved mother was completely worn out; she was forty-two years old when she passed away. Will distracted himself by noodling around an abandoned mine and much to his surprise, discovered a vein of silver. The more he dug, the bigger it got. For whatever reason, Will knew with certainty he was going to strike it rich and he delayed his return to Columbia. Not long after, when he should have been completing the sophomore fall semester, the vein of silver pinched-out and disappeared; perhaps he felt he'd made a big mistake. However, his New York dreams were far from over and the east still pulled at his heart.

"By now Will's father was involved in mining too; he took a chance and placed William in charge of his Boulder Chief silver mine in the mountains, about thirty miles northeast of Butte. But winter was approaching and the conditions became severe; Will almost froze to death and one of the younger workers was not as lucky. A short time later, the elder Thompson sold the underperforming mine, and though not fair, it appears his son was blamed for this failure.

"Will was completely fed up with mining; he took a break to visit the daughter of a Mississippi steamboat captain he'd met earlier in his travels. Apparently he was infatuated and it was rumored he was going to ask her to marry him. It turned out Captain Bixby's daughter had other plans and things did not go well on the trip. William returned to Butte very disheartened.

"By now the elder Thompson had invested in a lumber company in Helena, Montana and he decided to take another chance on his son. Will agreed to the relocation and served as the manager; he loved Helena because it reminded him of Alder Gulch in spirit and beauty.

"Bobbi, guess what happened while William was in Helena? I'm sure it was predictable. Even though he'd declared he was done with mining, there was a rumor about a secret copper mine near town that was for sale; of course he investigated further. This time he was certain he was finally going to hit the jackpot. He approached his father for financial help and before a homesick mole could find a hole, he became the owner of the Dutchman Mine in Helena

"It was at the entrance to his new acquisition where he met a rugged Ohio State graduate who was also a lumberman and a miner. His name was George Gunn and he had prior experience with Guggenheim-funded mining explorations; he knew what he was doing. Will made Gunn his superintendent and their hopes were high.

"Unfortunately the Dutchman Mine did not live up to expectations and Will's father was disappointed in his son yet again. The only positive thing that happened in the middle of this failure was that Will and George Gunn had formed a powerful friendship. They didn't know it yet, but their best years together were just around the corner.

"Will continued to supervise the lumberyard in Helena and he also managed a hardware store and a coal company. Gunn, for the time being, went his own way and became an ore-buyer for a smelting company.

"During the winter of 1895, William unexpectedly met, romanced and married Gertrude

Hickman. She was the daughter of another family from the south who had developed gold fever and also ended up in Alder Gulch a few years earlier. In fact at one point, the Hickmans had lived only a couple of hundred yards from the Thompsons and yet Will and Gertrude had never met.

"It was apparently a match made in heaven. One of my sources reported that the couple had a baby boy very early in their marriage; sadly he died as an infant. In 1897 they welcomed Margaret into the world and nicknamed her Peggy. She proved to be the twinkle in her father's eye and she was raised as an only child.

"During this time in Helena, Will caught the political bug and ran for the legislature as well as state treasurer. Unfortunately his stammering speech pattern and lack of charisma led to a dismal showing.

"Ultimately the Thompsons moved back to Butte from where Will continued to run the Helena businesses. However, in 1899, New York City was beckoning louder than ever and he threw all caution to the wind; Will informed his father he was quitting as manager of the Helena operations and moved his family across the country to Manhattan. He used his meager savings and rented a room at the Waldorf-Astoria until he could find a house.

I'm sure his father was dumbfounded and thought his son had lost his mind.

"Will promoted mines, bonds and everything else he could think of but he was not the instant sensation he thought he would be. The money ran out pretty quickly and his father propped up his ne'er-do-well son with profits from the family lumber business until his savings were almost drained too.

"It was during a period of desperation in 1900 that a casual acquaintance pointed Will in the direction of a virgin copper mine in Clifton, Arizona: the birthplace of Geronimo. He left his young family in New York and travelled across the country to set foot in Arizona for the first time. Negotiations to acquire the mine and surrounding holdings took him to Boston and Europe. His father, against his better judgment, was shamed by friends into helping with the financing. The mine took off and proved to be extremely profitable. Will finally had something of value to sell on the New York Stock Exchange; he was finally on his way.

"During this period of success, Will's father died quite suddenly and unexpectedly of a cerebral hemorrhage at 62 years of age. With the help of friends, Will had to secure financial backing all over again. There was no time to grieve.

"At about the same time, Will's old friend, George Gunn called him about an interesting prospect in Ely, Nevada and this acquisition also proved to be very profitable. This afforded Thompson an opportunity to become acquainted with Mr. William Smith who he hired to manage the Thompson electric, water and real estate companies that Will had started in Ely. Almost simultaneously, there were successful acquisitions in Mexico and a wildly profitable promotion of a silver-mine in Cobalt, Ontario, Canada.

"After years of failure, Thompson was suddenly an overnight success. He'd become a multi-millionaire and he and Gunn were just getting started. They purchased an under-performing mine in Miami, Arizona in 1907 and renamed it, Inspiration.

"Because everything was becoming quite complicated, Thompson required the help of a skilled California lawyer named Charles Ayer to sort out the legalities. Ayer became a trusted member of the team from that day forward. In 1912, William purchased the Silver Queen Mine near Superior and renamed it the Magma Mine. Sadly, it was the same year that Gunn passed away from long standing heart disease; once again there was no time to grieve.

"Thompson had now become fabulously wealthy. He owned and invested in mines all over the world and had become, 'The Power on Wall Street'. William, as he was now called, gave the appearance of a man on top of the world.

The Power on Wall Street
(BTA archives)

"However, something was amiss. He was smoking up to twenty cigars a day and eating excessively. William was overweight and being encouraged by friends to engage in some physical activity. He was bald and looked much older than his age."

I chose this moment to stop talking and Bobbi looked at me with a bewildered expression on her face. "Bobbi, I'm sorry to tell you this, but I need a break in order to collect my thoughts and organize my storytelling. I want to talk to some of my friends and check my facts. Don't you have something else to do for a couple of days? Also, it hasn't rained for a long time; I'm feeling dry and my thinking is sluggish."

"Gus, take whatever time you need. I know this has been an intense conversation. I think we could both use a time out."

With that being said, Bobbi stood up and poured the remaining containers of cold water on my feet and then walked down the hill and out of sight.

I closed my eyes and soaked in the ice water. It was a new sensation for me and I even experienced a momentary headache. However, it was refreshing and the ensuing silence was welcome; I think everyone needs some time to be still, and this was my time.

"The control of nature is a phrase conceived in arrogance, born of the Neanderthal age of biology and philosophy, when it was supposed that nature exists for the convenience of man."

Rachel Carson from *Silent Spring*

CHAPTER SEVEN

A COLONEL IS BORN

Not one of my friends at the arboretum had seen Bobbi in over two weeks and I was beginning to get worried. While I was eager to get on with the storytelling, I amused myself by watching the arboretum's ground crew perform their daily chores at my feet. Miguel drove by in his cart every morning and checked on the mescal bean bush he was particularly attached to. Becky and Tammy busily fixed the malfunctioning drip system in the Cactus Garden while Jeff pruned several nearby overgrown trees. George gathered the clippings and tossed them in the back of a white pickup truck. He was now in his twenty-seventh year of employment at the park and was personally responsible for planting more than five hundred specimens.

One morning I watched as Gonzalo walked slowly toward the administrative building, lost in his thoughts. He's one of many creative leaders of the crew and one can only guess about the new display he was dreaming about.

Volunteers were everywhere. Robert was collecting prickly pear fruit in order to make some punch for an upcoming educational event. Jim was talking about medicinal plants to a group from a local Buddhist temple while others were busy watering thirsty plants in the hummingbird garden. Another volunteer called Laura was continuing her quest to remove every single crayfish from Ayer Lake.

After much anticipation an entertainer and herpetologist, 'Wild Man' Phil, led a group on a lizard walk. His back pocket was bulging with the unmistakable shape of a regal horned lizard that would soon be part of his presentation. Several days later Sylvia, the arboretum's official historian, strode by telling her stories to an engaged audience. Randy and his crew from Game and Fish were setting up for another evening of bat catching; Adrienne, Ron, Gail and others gathered on the weekend to count butterflies as part of a national census exercise.

And yet there was still no sign of Bobbi and I began to fear she was gone forever.

The place was hopping and even a rain storm lingered overhead; I heard that two visitor center employees, Lynnae and Preston, were passing out umbrellas to the die-hard patrons. Even the administrators were visible. Gaylyn, the acting arboretum director, drove by in her buggy that was loaded with bait; she was on her way to catch several turkey vultures and fit them with radio transmitters to study their upcoming migration. Lacey was stressing about how to keep all the balls in the air now that Paul had retired from his position as volunteer coordinator.

I finally saw Bobbi out of the corner of my eye one Sunday morning, leading a group of Minnesota visitors around the park. She had her usual wide-brimmed green hat on and she looked up and waved to me as she walked by. I didn't know whether to feel relieved or angry. Two hours later, Bobbi was at my side again.

"Where in the world have you been? I was worried sick and I thought you didn't want to talk to me anymore."

"Gus, I've been really busy. I had patients to see in Gold Canyon; my mother needed help moving to her new assisted living facility up in Canada; I also had landscaping and a pool clean up to do and a few golf balls to hit. I needed to relax a little. Are you ready to get started again?"

"Of course I am. The last time we talked, Thompson had just purchased the Silver Queen

Mine that he had been leasing and he renamed it Magma Mine. The year was 1912."

"Gus, before we move forward, I want to tell you I've been rethinking this entire project. I want to be certain that William's biography is not going to be the retelling of another rag to riches story? There are already too many similar tales. I also don't have any interest in hearing about yet another American tycoon and their boastful adventures as they stride dismissively through life buying whatever bauble that strikes their fancy. I hope there is something different and really compelling about this fellow called Thompson? I want to write a book about someone people will actually be interested in."

"Oh, I see. You want someone compelling. Somebody that is different. Well hold on to your hat because it doesn't get any more special than the rest of thc story about William Boyce Thompson. Put your pen to your paper and let's get going.

"As the owner of Magma Mine, William Boyce Thompson did something radical. He was determined not to use wood-fired steam engines to power the mining equipment because he knew what the denuded, treeless landscape would look like. He did not want to create another Butte by robbing the Superior residents of their beautiful surrounding hillsides. Instead he used more expensive electric-powered engines. He obtained the electricity by stringing lines over rugged terrain from Miami to the Magma Mine, many miles away. Of course this dramatically cut into profits.

"Thompson also didn't utilize the usual approach of open-pit mining that gutted the countryside. Instead, he tunneled for the copper. There appeared to be a moral imperative to protect the environment as much as possible.

"His first inspection of Magma required a long journey from the east coast by train. He eventually arrived in Miami, Arizona, and completed the trip on horseback along a pathway to the mine.

"At that time, everything had to be brought to and from Magma using wagons along a nearby road that was both primitive and serpentine. Thompson found this transportation solution unacceptable and discussed plans to build a narrow-gauge railway line from the mine, through Superior, where it would eventually join the Southern Pacific at a junction northwest of Florence. He would call his narrow-gauge line the Magma Railroad.

"He also found time to explore the high country above Superior on horseback, like he was a kid again. He came to a place where he could look out at Queen Creek meandering through the unbelievably rugged but beautiful countryside below until finally disappearing from view. He was enchanted and felt the urge to make this place his home; he knew he would be back.

"Upon his return to New York, William regaled his wife and young daughter with stories about the spectacular cactus and wildlife in Arizona. However, he had to get back to the business of building a house for them. It wasn't going to be just a house. It was going to be a mansion: he was making a statement.

"The perfect lot was chosen on a bluff backing on to the Hudson River in Yonkers, New York. The architects, Carrere and Hastings, created a renaissance revival masterpiece for William and his wife and Thompson became the micromanager of all time. He weighed in on every detail, including the swirl in the marble that was selected. When he really cared about something, he had to constantly insert himself and be completely present. If a project was simply business as usual, like a mine, he would sit back, trust and delegate.

"Their home featured spectacular botanical gardens and he called the mansion Alder Manor. Alder was a word he reserved for his most cherished possessions because it reminded him of the happiest, most carefree days of his life, when he was a kid in Alder Gulch.

"When Thompson really treasured something, there were definite clues. Either he was micro-managing, or he used the names Alder or Boyce Thompson, in honor of his parents. If those two boxes are checked, the project was of paramount importance to him.

"Aside from the Alder Manor construction, he organized a brokerage house named Newmont Mining Corporation with the help of Charles Ayer. This associate proved invaluable as his mine holdings and speculation continued to grow.

"Because William experienced multiple successes in a row, people were now flocking to him with the latest information on the most appealing mines all over the world. He was making an absolute fortune and a boastful story, circulated by family members, claimed that William once had the opportunity to purchase half of the land that is now Los Angeles. Given the contacts he had, it is entirely plausible. Such a purchase would have made him wealthy beyond imagination. However, as the story goes, he turned the opportunity down because the venture speculated on land and homes; he felt there was something immoral about hedging on things as necessary as homes in the interest of making a profit. He'd already tried that once in Ely, Nevada and it had left a bad taste.

"He became a member of the Rocky Mountain Club and took pride in contributing to its philanthropic work. He donated liberally to Phillips Exeter Academy, libraries, parks and humanitarian relief work in Belgium. It was through charitable work that he became friends with Herbert Hoover, Chairman of the American Relief Commission.

"It was Hoover who made him aware of the humanitarian crisis in Russia after the revolution and William agreed to fund and travel with the Red Cross relief effort in 1917. He was given the title of Colonel as a result of this endeavor: The Red Cross was a division of the military at the time.

"President Woodrow Wilson became aware of the mission and met with Thompson to explore whether he would be willing to secretly meet behind the scenes with Russian power players and officials. At the time, the United States was interested in moving the chaotic post-revolution political scene in the direction of democracy, if at all possible. Thompson agreed and clandestine meetings took place. However, they did not progress in the direction that Wilson hoped and this led to friction and unresolved arguments between the two of them.

"While in Russia, Thompson had an experience that changed the purpose of his life forever. He witnessed starvation in all of its ugliness and it shook him to his core. It was at that moment he made another life promise to himself.

"He vowed that on return to America, he would make certain no one in the world went hungry again. I'm sure others must have thought this pie-in-the-sky proclamation was simply an example of hubris run wild. However, Thompson was not fooling around. Given his interest in science and especially botany, he dreamed of assembling the best scientists and tasking them with developing new and improved crops that would thrive in hard-to-grow regions. Yields would be increased; people everywhere would have access to these new technologies and be able to feed and clothe themselves; they'd also have something left over to sell; they would be secure in one of the most fundamental human needs.

"So what do you think now, Bobbi? Is this man called Thompson interesting enough for you or do you think he is just another boring multi-millionaire? Is he a compelling enough subject for your book, or would you like to pass?"

"Well, he's not your average tycoon, that's for sure. He is an incredibly complex and likeable character who works hard and dreams big. This is fantastic stuff, Gus. Please continue."

"Man can and must prevent the tragedy of famine in the future instead of merely trying with pious regret to salvage the human wreckage of the famine, as he has so often done in the past."

Norman Borlaug

"Conservation is a state of harmony between man and land."

Aldo Leopold

"The one process now going on that will take millions of years to correct is the loss of genetics and species by the destruction of natural habitats. This is the folly our descendants are least likely to forgive us."

E. O. Wilson

CHAPTER EIGHT

THE RENAISSANCE MAN

Thompson returned from Russia to Yonkers and as promised, set in motion his grand plan to end starvation. Thompson created the Boyce Thompson Institute for Plant Research in honor of his long-deceased parents. His goals were to better understand plants, improve the world food supply and promote conservation. This undertaking was of paramount importance; it was too special to turn over to a university outside of his immediate reach and control. Instead he purchased property across the street from Alder Manor and constructed a state of the art laboratory, teaching facility, and greenhouses in which to conduct experiments. He hired the best botanists he could find and by the early 1920s, everything was up and running under his ever watchful eye.

Of course he still had his mining empire to run and this required a great deal of travel. At one time or another he also promoted the Indian Motorcycle company, Sinclair Oil and Cuba Cane Sugar. He helped organize Wright-Martin Aircraft. Aside from that, he controlled Pierce Arrow Motor Car Company and sat on various boards. To say the least, he was driven.

In 1921, he made another life-altering decision, this time involving his health. William had struggled with obesity for years and secretly consulted a surgeon about weight-loss surgery. It appeared he desired a very personal physical renaissance and revival in keeping with the theme of Alder Manor. As was typical of the extremely wealthy at the time, he had installed a state-of-the-art surgical facility in his mansion; his surgery was performed at the house.

"Bobbi, the historians have not been able to find any operative reports. However, given the fact you are a medical doctor, what type of procedure would likely have been performed?"

"To my knowledge, Gus, bypass surgical approaches were only invented in the 1950s; I am almost positive he would not have had a diverting procedure. However, there were attempts made to scoop fat deposits away with the use of incisions and curettes in the early 1920s. I believe it was a surgeon in France who developed this technique; complications were severe including death or, in one case, the amputation of a leg. Given Thompson's wealth and connections, I wonder if he would have sent for Dr. Dujarrier, a Parisian, to perform the operation."

"Well that's very interesting and it appears there were complications of some sort. William was 52 years old at the time and after the procedure, he suffered from some ill-defined, lingering condition for the rest of his life.

"His physical renaissance may have fallen short of expectations, but it did not prevent William from continuing his punishing work schedule. Thompson was back in Arizona that same year to check out his Magma Mine. He also had another project in mind: William wanted to build a winter vacation home in Arizona; he began the search for the perfect site.

"Bobbi, I remember the day like it was yesterday. We were all trying to recover from yet another long and blistering summer on Magma Ridge when, all of a sudden, every living thing in the garden started sounding the alarm: There was an intruder in our midst. The Bell's vireo family was the first to spot a group of five men looking over the cliff just east of where I stand; their horses stood calmly nearby, munching on some grama grass. One of the men was wearing a long black coat. He was somewhat short and stocky and peered over glasses perched on the tip of his nose. He was obviously the leader and he gestured and pointed in a very purposeful manner. There was no way to hear what they were talking about. The meeting lasted almost an hour and as the minutes passed, we became gripped by a feeling of dread; there was a collective sense that something really awful was about to happen and none of us could speak.

"At last the men rode off to the east in a cloud of dust. It was a sleepless night for all in this tight-knit community."

*"Your deepest roots are in nature,
no matter who you are, where you live, or what kind of life you lead. You remain irrevocably linked with the rest of creation."*

C. Cook

"When you are up against a wall, put down roots like a tree, until clarity comes from deeper sources, to see over that wall and grow."

C. G. Jung

"To move freely, one must be deeply rooted."

Anonymous

CHAPTER NINE

PUTTING DOWN ROOTS

The next morning the men were gone but not forgotten. The best furry and feathered reporters were dispatched in all directions to find out what was going on. Several days later a special meeting was convened on Magma Ridge and there was a record attendance. We had learned that the chubby man in the coat, who appeared to be the leader, was visiting from New York. His name was Colonel William Boyce Thompson and he was the owner of the copper mine in Superior. Apparently he was looking for a place to build a smelter for his mine.

A tiny pocket mouse called Pee Wee was standing at my feet and he asked, in his innocent little voice, "What's a smelter?"

A large raven, named Ronnie, cleared his throat and answered, "Smelting is used to get the copper out of the rocks they are mining up there. They heat up the rocks until they are red-hot and then apply chemicals to separate the copper from the stuff they don't want. It causes the release of dangerous rotten egg smelling chemicals into the air and everyone starts coughing and gagging. The mucky, poisonous sludge left over runs down to holding areas where it sits and rots forever and ever. That's what smelting is all about."

The entire assembly gasped. No one could speak. Then the leopard frogs started to cry and others joined in. As everyone was leaving, lost in their thoughts, I cautioned the community to remain calm until we could verify this information. The anxiety was palpable.

Several days went by, and then weeks; after a few months passed with no further sightings of the Colonel, we all started to breathe more easily. Perhaps another location had been chosen for their smelter. It was now 1922 and the state highway just to the north had been completed. The Clevengers were still living here and they had been joined by a few other homesteaders who built equally primitive shelters around the area. Life was quietly humming along.

And then without any warning, he was back. This William Boyce Thompson was standing in the same spot and was once again pointing and drawing pictures in the dirt with his cane. Several rock wrens flew, with the utmost of stealth, to a bush nearby and listened to every word. They reported back to me immediately and I convened another town hall that very evening.

I bellowed to the noisy crowd. "Can I have your attention? Would everyone sit down and be quiet." I was screaming, but no one was listening. At that point all the rock wrens started to call in unison, using their best imitation of referee whistles; they finally got everyone's attention and I could make my announcement: "Thank you for coming. Thank you. I have some news. Please sit down."

You could have heard a legume pod drop.

"I know you are all anxious to hear about what is going on at the overlook. Several informants secretly attended the meeting this morning involving William Boyce Thompson and his staff. I have some very good news. They will not be building a smelter here. Let me repeat. There will be no smelter built in our neighborhood."

The joyous screaming and shouting that followed was deafening. Once order was restored, I continued. "He has already built the smelter near the mine in Superior. However, Thompson is going to build a structure on the bluff; it's going to be a wonderful house for him and his wife, Gertrude; he dreams their daughter, Margaret, and their two grandchildren will visit too. And that's not all. He intends to make this entire area a beautiful and protected garden for people to enjoy from far and wide. He also wants scientists to perform research here to find out how plants grow best. Finally, he hopes this great garden of his will become a place where people can come to learn."

After I stopped speaking, there was more applause and dancing in the creek. It was one of the most amazing moments of my life.

It did not take long for Thompson to get the project underway. The land chosen to build the house upon was part of Crook's National Forest. In order to secure the land he wanted, the Colonel had to arrange a complicated exchange of another property bought to the north of Magma Mines. The properties owned by the Clevengers and several other homesteaders were also purchased.

There was frenetic activity in all directions. The construction of the Mediterranean style home was begun in the spring of 1923 and completed in the fall. Plans for the new botanical garden were well underway. The decision to convert the nearby narrow gauge railway line to standard gauge was also made; once completed, this would allow the

Thompsons to travel all the way from New York in their private rail car and park at a siding they would create, about a half mile from the house.

William Boyce Thompson was really putting down roots in Arizona.

It might not have been where he was born, but it was going to be where he chose to live. He had fallen victim to the states enormous charm. He debated over what to name the new dwelling and for the longest time he called it the Thompson Ranch House. Everyone else called it Picket Post House and gradually the name stuck.

"Bobbi, I'm surprised he didn't name it Alder Manor West."

"Well I'm not surprised at all," Bobbi said. "You've already told me that if the Colonel was completely captivated by a project, he micromanaged and named it either Alder or Boyce Thompson. There was no evidence of micromanagement going on here. Heck, he wasn't even present during the actual construction; to top it all off, the original blueprints did not include drawings for a functioning kitchen with cupboards and drawers and countertops. This was a glaring omission and meant the building plans had to be revised in the form of change orders after the construction was well underway. If he'd really been engaged in the process, Thompson would never have let that slip by.

"I also have a hunch that he and his wife never talked together about the plans, as evidenced by what happened when they moved into their new $20,000.00 house in October of 1923.

Picket Post House at the completion of construction, 1923 (BTA archives)

"Almost immediately problems arose: Mr. Thompson was an early riser and he was using a cane for some reason. He thumped around on the hardwood floors in the wee hours of the morning and awakened his wife who liked to sleep-in; this became a major point of friction and she demanded her own bedroom as far away as possible from the noise. The Colonel acquiesced and ordered a separate small house with a big bedroom be built to the east of the main house; this would become Mrs. Thompson's bedroom house.

"Then he realized he did not like sleeping in the main house because all the very necessary support staff was housed on the first floor and he required more privacy; he made plans to have his own bedroom constructed to the south of the main building. This became known as the Colonel's house. Construction of both new structures was commenced almost immediately: a remedial solution that could have been avoided had more thought gone in to the original concept. The opposite of micromanaging was going on with this project, but at least Thompson had plenty of money to smooth everything over.

"This is likely why the home wasn't called Alder"

"You've made some very interesting observations, Bobbi. We'll never know if your conclusions are correct. It makes me wonder if they were both really emotionally invested in this house to begin with.

"Here is one thing that is indisputable: Thompson was obsessed with planning the arboretum and pushing his new dream forward. Even though he returned to Yonkers in the spring of 1924, his heart remained in the cactus-studded hills and the rugged canyon he had temporarily left behind. And he named it Boyce Thompson Arboretum. This project really mattered."

CHAPTER TEN

THE DEVIL AND MRS. THOMPSON

Plans for the botanical garden were coming together in 1924. Thompson was successful in signing Mr. Franklin J. Crider to a contract as the first director of the Boyce Thompson South West Arboretum. Crider was a renowned University of Arizona botany professor with a passionate interest in the biology of roots and the adaptation of plants to life in arid lands.

Another U of A professor, Mr. Frederick Gibson, was chosen as assistant to Mr. Crider and became the second senior employee to sign a contract. Along with Thompson, this threesome shared their visions and solutions to problems on a daily basis. As a result of their collective genius, the first botanical garden west of the Mississippi was conceived. They discussed the routing of walking trails, irrigation lines and planting schemes.

A reliable source of water would be needed, and after many brain-storming sessions, the decision was made to construct a reservoir lake on the property.

The process became bumpy at times. The Colonel had strong feelings about which plants should be the focus of research at the arboretum, but Crider disagreed. This lead to some spirited conversations; if nothing else, this micromanaging by the Colonel was proof-positive about how much he cared about the undertaking.

Construction began and was completed on two new residences on the west side of the garden. They became known as the Crider and Gibson houses to allow these principle leaders to be on site at all times.

The Thompsons returned in the fall of 1924 to their winter home, or should I say homes.

View from the east revealing all the homes.
Upper left is the Colonel's. Upper right is the main house.
Foreground is Mrs. Thompson's house
(BTA archives)

The Colonel spent every waking moment enjoying the weather, the property and overseeing the work. It was decided to dig a deeper well beside the old Clevenger well along Queen Creek in order to secure large amounts of water needed for irrigation. Plans were drawn for the man-made lake, complete with a dam, and it would be located on the east side of the property. Propagation greenhouses, an administration building, a weather station and novel concrete structures with below ground viewing windows to study root development were all on the drawing-board. A trip was planned to the Baja peninsula to acquire the bizarre and newly discovered Boojum trees. They would certainly be a tourist attraction. Can you imagine the excitement and the creative energy that was bouncing everywhere off the canyon walls?

The Thompsons had another goal in mind. They wanted to entice their daughter and the grandchildren to visit this strange new place. Margaret was reluctant because of the danger that snakes could pose for her and the kids; the Colonel had elaborate, fine-mesh fencing constructed around Picket Post House to serve as a snake barrier. He further readied the home for their anticipated special guests by enclosing the outdoor veranda and creating an area for parties and dancing.

Thompson also dangled another carrot in front of the grandchildren by announcing he was going to build a play house for them. What he had in mind was modifying the old Clevenger house by adding a third room, a secure roof, a real floor and protective fencing.

As if that wasn't enough, he told them he was going to create a zoo. In fact the very next March, he took delivery of a brown bear that had been rescued by Arizona Game and Fish and housed it in a cage on the property. He also boasted he had pigs at the arboretum as well, though one could hardly call the wild, smelly peccaries as being part of a zoo.

Mrs. Thompson also became involved in a project of her own. As a benefactor of the American Museum of Natural History in New York, she had provided funding for several archeological expeditions. Now she was covering the cost to explore the Togetzoge Indian ruins east of the Magma Mine toward Globe, Arizona. Hopefully more artifacts would be discovered to allow for a better understanding of the culture and the people that had lived in the area about 800 years ago.

Gertrude Thompson
(Courtesy of Boyce Thompson)

There had already been explorations of cliff-dwellings in nearby Tonto basin. The entire area appeared to have been a melting pot where ancient

Pueblo, Sonoran Desert and Mogollon cultures had come together collectively as people of the Salado. These communities mysteriously disappeared several hundred years ago and perhaps the new expedition would unravel the reasons. Much later, the land was inhabited by nomadic hunter-gatherers including the Yavapai and Tonto Apaches. For the most part they got along, or at least tolerated one another, in spite of their different language and origin stories.

Mrs. Thompson must have enjoyed this activity because she took the time to visit the site and met some of the workers. One of the crew was a diminutive, hard-working Apache named Natchilta. He was from the San Carlos reservation and apparently served as a tribal doctor; he had an extensive knowledge of medicinal plants. He was also called Tsling: the devil. It is spiritually forbidden in the Apache culture to disturb the dead and because he was engaged in exhuming bodies at the ruins, he was considered to be doing Satan's work. In any event, Mrs. Thompson must have found this devil very intriguing because she hired Natchilta to design and plant the gardens around Picket Post House.

Gertrude had no way of knowing the significance of what she had done. She had just allowed a powerful personality access to their property and there would be long-lasting consequences.

"Gus, you have done it again. I'm on the edge of my seat because you've introduced this mysterious character into the arboretum story; I have a feeling this is going to be good."

"Bobbi, get a fresh pen and more note paper; hold on to your seat, because everything is about to get even more exciting. Now don't interrupt me."

"The only way to have a friend is to be one."

Ralph Waldo Emerson

"Ultimately the bond of all companionship
whether in marriage or in friendship
is conversation."

Oscar Wilde

"Be true to your work, your word and your friends."

Henry David Thoreau

CHAPTER ELEVEN

THE MEDICINE MAN

Natchilta was perhaps five feet tall on a good day and he was known by the locals as Nat Patterson. He was born on August 22, 1885 in San Carlos and learned a great deal about construction, equipment operation and wall building while working on the Roosevelt Dam project when he was 20 years old. Later he was a member of the general work crew during the construction of the Phelps Dodge smelter in Clarkdale.

Nat Patterson
(BTA archives)

Natchilta had developed an extensive knowledge of medicinal plants from his elders on the reservation and was regarded as one of several tribal medicine men. The jojoba was his specialty and he readily shared his recipe for extracting oil from the seed in order to heal skin ulcers and abrasions.

It did not take the Colonel long to notice him working in the house gardens. Nat had a strong work ethic and he was clever; he helped Thompson construct the snake fencing around the perimeter of the main house and the play house on Queen Creek. He also, with the help of others, created small rock-and-mortar "flower boxes" on the lava walls surrounding Picket Post so the Colonel would have a place to plant his favorite specimens.

Friendships are mysterious things and sometimes they develop between the most unlikely individuals. It became very clear that William Boyce Thompson liked Nat and the feeling was mutual. Thompson hired him as one of the first ground crew employees in February of 1925 and he allowed him to live onsite. In fact he gave permission for Nat to build a house a few hundred feet east of Picket Post. Calling it a house was an exaggeration because the adobe structure had a tin roof, a dirt floor, no electricity, toilet or running water. The Colonel, in an act of generosity, directed water from the big house to a spigot beside the hut. This simple shelter might not have been pretty, but it was home for Nat and his wife, Fanny, and their son, Morgan. They had several dogs and cats to keep the snakes away and Thompson especially enjoyed having these pets nearby, given he was never allowed this pleasure as a youngster.

The medicine man was tasked with all kinds of projects. He built the large stone-framed sign announcing the arboretum to the public. Gibson directed him to construct the irrigation system and build trails; Nat helped clear the land and remove debris in preparation for the planting of specimens.

He was often seen walking the property with the Colonel while the boss pointed out the exact placement for plants.

The Colonel, with cane in hand, pointing to a specimen (BTA archive)

It became obvious that Nat was gifted; he could build anything and operate all the equipment; he was ingenious and his problem-solving abilities were unmatched.

Of course help was needed as construction proceeded and Thompson asked Nat to find more laborers. He quickly recruited Apache friends and the Colonel allowed them to build huts and live on the property next to Nat as well. This was yet another welcoming gesture on Thompson's part, given the historical tension between the white settlers and indigenous people. The area became known as the Indian Village.

Fanny Patterson also provided invaluable help to the Gibson family by minding their daughter, Kaytee. Fanny and Nat also helped Kaytee care for the horse she was allowed to keep in the Thompson carriage house, not far from Picket Post.

When the Thompsons departed for New York in the spring of 1925, they left a beehive of activity behind. The Colonel had business to attend to in South Africa where a big trip was planned in order to evaluate another mine investment. They were barely out of sight in April when the construction of the new Queen Creek well was commenced and renovations to the Clevenger house were started. Mr. Crider left on a trip to the Baja area of Mexico to acquire many plants, including the aforementioned Boojum trees.

When Crider returned with the Boojums, Nat was speechless: the specimens looked like giant carrots turned upside down in their boxes and thorny branches stuck out horizontally in all directions.

The story of naming these bizarre plants was as convoluted as the way in which they were discovered. It starts with Professor Godfrey Sykes, a botanist working at the Desert Lab for Plant Research in Tucson in the early 1920s. One of his sons, while working as a hunting guide in the Baja, had his picture taken after swimming in the Sea of Cortez. He returned to Tucson and shared the photo with his father who took immediate notice of a strange tree in the background.

A return trip was organized and the son guided his father to the forest of these surreal trees. Professor Sykes was initially silent and then he exclaimed, "I think we have found the Boojum!"

The Boojum was a mysterious, elusive creature who was always just out of sight in a popular Lewis Carroll poem at the time called *The Hunting of the Snark*. Apparently Sykes had recently read the poem and Boojum was on his mind: the name fit the tree perfectly. Sykes was well known to Crider and Gibson and they developed "Boojum envy" and had to acquire specimens of the weird tree for the arboretum: Nat and others had the pleasure of planting them.

Nat Patterson, far left

(BTA archive)

The well was successfully drilled and a dam was constructed to contain water in the new reservoir called Ayer Lake, named in honor of the Colonel's long-standing lawyer and business associate. Nat and the rest of the construction crew were shaken to their core when Mexican Slim, one of their co-workers, drowned in the newly filled lake. Every big dream exacts a human price and this was no exception.

On a personal note, I'll never forget the morning I awoke from a restful night of sleep, looked to my right, and was surprised to see the lake. The surface was smooth as glass and the reds and yellows of the sunrise were reflected in the water. It was stunning and every morning since, I've looked forward with added excitement to the sun coming up. I can even see swallows, purple martins and black phoebes zooming above the surface if I squint just so. I remember the day that Arizona Game and Fish arrived and stocked the lake with perch, catfish and Missouri Channel fish.

To everyone's surprise, the Colonel added an alligator to the lake a year later as part of his private zoo. I'm not sure the fish were happy with this arrangement but, on balance, the reservoir enriched everyone's life around here and I bow, as much as a saguaro can bow, and thank the Colonel every day.

Touched by this reflective moment, Bobbi spoke up and said, "Gus, if I didn't know better, I'd swear you are becoming sentimental. Do you need some Kleenex? If you want to stop now, I can come back early tomorrow morning. If not, then let's push forward and preserve your train of thought."

"I'm all right Bobbi. Do you have any extra water you could share with me so I could freshen up a little?"

Bobbi poured a bottle of chilled water on my feet and within a minute, I was fully alert and ready to go again.

"Great talents are the most lovely and often the most dangerous fruits on the tree of humanity. They hang upon the most slender twigs that are easily snapped off."

Carl Jung

CHAPTER TWELVE

PREDICTABLE

While the well, the lake and the Boojum projects were going on, the Thompsons completed their cross country journey back to Alder Manor. Before you could blink, the Colonel was on his way to visit Phillips Exeter Academy. It was not the last time he would be drawn back to his childhood place of learning. This time he learned the salaries the teachers were receiving was not in keeping with their training and expertise and he gave them all bonuses. He also learned there were other important programs that were falling short because of the lack of equipment and space. He responded by donating money for a fully-equipped science building; an administration center; a gymnasium; a pool and baseball cages, squash courts, dormitories and the like. He also threw in another million dollars and reminded the admissions office that they must not ignore accepting the poor student because he himself was once poor.

Thompson and his wife left for South Africa: he was considering investing in gold and diamond mines. Halfway there, he became ill and stopped in France where he recovered. The nature of his malady remains unknown. However, it was significant enough to require cancellation of the larger trip and they returned home.

Following several months of recovery, the Colonel and his wife returned to Picket Post in the fall of 1925. They did it in style this time because he had commissioned a customized Pullman rail car; of course he called it *Alder*. They travelled with their support staff and the colored help was in tow, in a regular Pullman car. Thompson's narrow-gauge railway line had been replaced with standard rail allowing them to continue from the Southern Pacific, up the Magma Railroad to a siding not far from the arboretum. They were greeted by his courteous driver and ferried in their luxurious Pierce Arrow automobile to the house, a half a mile away. The white staff was also driven to Picket Post where they resided on the first floor; the non-white staff wasn't allowed to ride in the car and had to walk to the house every morning and back to their

Pullman at night where they slept. This was the law back in the day.

Thompson quickly became reengaged with Crider and Gibson and sought out Nat as well. He asked how the crew was doing and was informed that one of the Apache was injured and had to return to San Carlos. The Colonel was concerned and offered to help in any way, even if it was financial.

He walked the newly created trails with Nat and had some pathways redirected so as not to disturb preexisting native plants. He also allowed Patterson to plant a garden of his own and designated a plot of land near the confluence of Queen Creek and Silver King Wash for Nat's use only. He trusted Patterson completely and it was Nat who placed some of the first orders for seed on behalf of the arboretum.

The staff created a vegetable garden near the old Clevenger house for the Thompsons to use. Almost daily, new plants and seeds arrived from all over the world. There were pines from Palestine; forage plants from Morocco; rare fruits from Persia; and arid-climate plants from Australia, South America and South Africa. Thompson, ever the dreamer, was hopeful that perhaps one of these plants, or a hybrid, would change everything for world food production. Patterson and the crew were constantly planting under the direction of Crider and Gibson. Nat was the irrigation expert and he made certain everything was well-watered, especially the medicinal plants he so loved and was most familiar with.

The Colonel got along with other common folk too. For example, he befriended Doby Tom, a former sailor from Slovakia. Apparently Doby was responsible for the sinking of a boat he piloted while intoxicated: a mistake that ended his career as a sailor. He had reinvented himself as a stone mason in the desert, but he continued to be a character who swore like he was still at sea. He and the Colonel often engaged in verbal sparring matches; it was all in good fun.

Thompson would "mess" with Doby while he was hard at work building a stone wall. For example, during a spasm of micromanagement, he would ask him to reposition a stone in a wall every which way and sideways. Doby would laugh and laugh and comply with the absurdity. He was lighthearted and patient and the two of them became an odd couple. The Colonel would bait and tease him and Doby would curse and dish it right back with a smile; he played pranks on his boss in playful retaliation. It was Doby who constructed the retaining wall below Picket Post House: a wall that has remained solid for over ninety years.

One day, the conversation became quite serious when the Colonel shared with Nat and Doby that his father had died of a stroke many years before at the age of 62. He told them he feared paralysis would be his undoing too and instructed them to create ramps so he would be able to get around the park in the future when he was infirm. They did not know what to make of his morbid instructions and the matter was never discussed again.

Construction of the new lab and administration building was started in late November of 1925. There was great excitement when it was announced that the New York Botanical Garden was donating their Britton cactus collection to the arboretum. This was followed by another donation: the Smithsonian's Rose cactus garden. Mr. Crider travelled to New York to organize the complicated process of shipping these specimens back to Arizona. The arboretum was now being contacted by botanists from all over the world and it must have been a heady time for Thompson and his staff.

Decisions were being made about which regions of the world to feature at the arboretum. For certain, there would be South American, Mediterranean, African and Australian-themed areas; well over two thousand species would be planted.

Winter eased into spring and the Thompsons were on their way back to Alder Manor again. The Colonel left behind organized chaos. He also left behind a very grateful William Smith.

To refresh your memory, Mr. Smith had been hired many years before to manage the Colonel's water, electric and real estate businesses in Ely, Nevada. It appears that Thompson wanted to help his friend actually acquire these interests. However, Smith did not have sufficient savings to obtain a loan; the Colonel waived a down payment and simply allowed him to make the purchase over time using the profits from the businesses. Mr. Smith was overjoyed at this gesture of generosity.

Later on, the Colonel informed William Smith that he had made adjustments to his will; when he died, Smith would inherit the businesses free and clear. Mr. Smith was dumbfounded.

Once again the essence of William Boyce Thompson was on full display. He was generous to a fault, although he was often heard saying, "For my friends, yes; for my friends' friends, no."

The Colonel was back in Yonkers in the spring and summer of 1926. He visited Exeter again but felt ill and immediately retired to bed where he requested the staff find some of his original school books to read. He was in a reflective mood when he met Lamont, an old school friend, and it appears that Lamont realized his spirits were low. He told the Colonel he had nominated him as a trustee of Phillips Exeter. Lamont had underestimated how much this gesture meant to the Colonel whose gloom seemed to visibly disappear.

When Mr. and Mrs. Thompson travelled back to the arboretum in early autumn, there was a spring in the Colonel's step. He walked the trails with Nat and checked out the new plantings. There was a new road being built connecting the administration building with Picket Post House and he obsessed about its routing and grading.

Thompson was walking more than he had in months and then the predictable happened. A combination of family history, cigar-smoking, an insane work schedule, stress, and over-eating collided and there was nothing to be done at the eleventh hour to stop its conclusion.

He awoke on the morning of October 22, 1926 and discovered his left side was paralyzed. He was 57 years old and five years younger than his father, when he succumbed to a brain bleed. At least Thompson's stroke did not appear to be hemorrhagic. His servant was the first to discover the Colonel was in trouble; Mrs. Thompson was notified and a doctor was summoned from Superior. Treatment was limited to measures of support and comfort.

The news spread through the arboretum like a lightning bolt. Rumors of his impending demise rattled his financial holdings. However, little by little the Colonel gained strength and by the tenth day he was out in the arboretum, being pushed about in a wheelchair by aides; with Nat at his side.

His doctors insisted he immediately travel to his southern residence in Palm Beach, Florida where the weather was warmer and there was more medical expertise available. Thompson objected but he was not in charge anymore. To make matters worse, he was banned from eating fattening foods or smoking cigars. What kind of new life would this be for the Colonel?

As he was being prepared for the long trip to Florida, he reassured everyone at the arboretum that he would be back. He waved goodbye, boarded the train and now became a prisoner of doctors, nurses, therapists and dieticians. He had a lot of thinking to do.

CHAPTER THIRTEEN

Loose Ends

After spending the winter in Florida, the Colonel ultimately made it back to Alder Manor. He slowly gained strength. However, his left side remained paralyzed and his voice was reduced to a hoarse whisper. Because his future was uncertain, there was no time to waste. He made modifications to his will to ensure that ownership of Picket Post House and the arboretum was changed from Magma Mines to the newly created Boyce Thompson Southwestern Foundation. Thompson set aside money in order that the arboretum could be funded for years to come.

A year after his stroke, he and his wife returned to the arboretum; Thompson's ongoing paralysis prevented him from gaining access to his personal bedroom house. Instead, they stayed in the main Picket Post House and he experienced great difficulty navigating the stairs and narrow doorways in a wheelchair.

Back in Yonkers in early 1928, Thompson met with Dr. Townsend of the New York Zoological Society, who was concerned that the Galapagos Island tortoises were in danger of extinction. Thousands had been slaughtered for food by visiting merchant ship sailors. He convinced the Colonel to provide refuge for 19 young tortoises and arrangements were made to have them shipped to the arboretum. An elaborate enclosure, wading pond and hibernaculum were constructed and the exotic creatures arrived in May of 1928. At the time they each weighed fifty pounds, but once they reached adult size, they would tip the scales at seven hundred pounds.

The Colonel could not wait to get back to Arizona the following winter to see the tortoises, the brown bear, and of course the alligator. Once again he wrote to his granddaughter, encouraging her to come with her brother and see all the magical things he had prepared for them.

However, he did not want to experience the physical challenge that Picket Post House had presented a year before; he and his wife stayed at a location in Phoenix from where they visited the arboretum daily. This decision proved equally unsatisfactory because he was sixty miles from the crew and the action; he felt completely disconnected.

In a moment of frustration, he instructed that his bedroom house be torn down and reconstructed with an elevator, rooms for a doctor and aides and even larger windows overlooking Queen Creek. When he returned in the future, he would be on-site again where he could participate more fully.

All was not work: Thompson owned several yachts and loved to be piloted around the east coast and enjoy the simple pleasure of the wind in his face and the waves lapping against the boat. This provided the peace and quiet he apparently treasured so much. In the summer of 1929, he purchased an even larger yacht and this would be his final act of extravagance. The ship was called the *Savarona* and at 294 feet, it was the second largest yacht in the world. He assembled a crew and set forth on a luxurious Mediterranean cruise. Of course, he renamed the ship Alder.

Family members were on board as they sailed along the Riviera and visited Naples, Corsica, Crete and Athens. Arthur Smith, the son of his old friend William, accompanied the Colonel and read to him as the shoreline drifted by.

Eventually he sailed back across the Atlantic and docked in Miami early in 1930, after the stock market had crashed. However, Thompson had other things on his mind: he wanted to visit Arizona again.

In March, he made his way back to the arboretum and his newly rebuilt, three-storey bedroom house. He had to be wheeled along a path around the west side of Picket Post House where a huge rock outcropping encroached on the pathway, the base of which had to be dynamited to allow clearance for the wheelchair.

He enjoyed seeing Crider, Gibson and the rest of the staff again and marveled at the progress that had been made; he delighted in being pushed along the paths as he greeted arboretum guests. He also reveled in observing two sunsets every evening: he would sit in his wheelchair on the ground floor of the house, and as the sun set, he would have his attendant load him into the elevator and send him to the top floor where he could watch it all over again.

After his stroke, Thompson placed his flaccid left hand in his pants pocket, likely to support the arm and also to reduce the appearance of disability. It took great effort for him to stand as his balance was now precarious.
(BTA archive)

He resumed teasing his old friend, Doby. He ordered him to pan for gold in Queen Creek in full view of the Colonel, who watched laughing from his bedroom. Of course there was no gold in the creek: Doby played along.

In a bittersweet moment, he was wheeled down to the Clevenger playhouse where it sat waiting to be filled with the sound of children's laughter. His daughter and the grandchildren were nowhere to be seen; they never would make the trip.

Thompson now looked like a very old and broken man and his voice was barely audible. The tortoises were not doing well either. Three had died of pneumonia; they were not built for the cold of the desert winter or the lack of humidity and they had no use for the burrows because they had not evolved where hibernation was required.

The entire tortoise rescue operation had been ill-conceived. Like the old Chinese proverb about saving fish from drowning, no matter how early the Samaritan arrived at the sea to remove the fish from the water and place them on the beach, they would all die, day after day. It was assumed they had drowned from being in the water too long. Even the most well-intentioned acts can often result in disaster; it was the tortoises that paid the price this time.

Thompson made it back to Alder Manor in May as the flowers in his garden were exploding back to life. Though it was the season for renewal, William Boyce Thompson died on June 27, 1930. The cause of death was pneumonia. He was sixty-one years of age and he lived one year less than his father and nine years less than Robert Clevenger. Are there any lessons to be learned here?

CHAPTER FOURTEEN

THE REST OF THE STORY

"I think we've come to the end, Bobbi. You wanted to write a book about the Colonel and the early years of the arboretum. I have told you everything I know. Bobbi? Bobbi?"

Gus turned to look and saw her sitting in exactly the same spot she had sat for weeks now. Her briefcase was at her feet and a pen and notebook were on her lap. She was crying.

"Bobbi! My dear friend, what's the matter?"

"Oh, Gus, it's just so sad. The whole thing is just so darned sad. His life was cut short and I fear the vision and daring of this arboretum was cut short too. Of course I already knew how the Colonel died before I started writing the book. However, listening to you tell the story simply got to me. Isn't it ironic that when we began this project, you were the one crying about Hope and now at the end,

I am the one blubbering about Thompson? We make a very watery pair."

"It is sad, Bobbi. He was so young. I've been doing a lot of thinking too. I know you're a doctor and I have wanted to ask you this question for a long time. Was there something that could have been done to prevent this? And why did he drive himself so? Do you have any idea what made him tick, Bobbi?"

"Gus, do you really want to hear the conclusions I've come to about the Colonel?" Gus nodded yes.

"Well okay and here we go. Remember: I'm a family physician and not a psychologist. However, during my training, I was taught about family dynamics and how a unit can function well…or not. Perhaps you will find this helpful because I know individuals at the arboretum ask you for advice all the time.

"This will be brief and over-simplified. To begin with, young Will was the oldest child of a very large family. The very fact that he was first placed a certain amount of pressure on him. Like it or not, he was expected to be the standard-bearer for the family: the star; the best that William and Anne could produce.

"Second, every youngster, including Will, has to feel they are treasured and unconditionally loved, no matter what. In the case of this family, his father was mostly absent. This was likely not by intent but simply the reality of how hard he had to work and how many mouths he had to feed. When he was around, he was emotionally distant. He scolded Will for being lazy, forbade him from having a pet, mocked him for using hand cream and reminded everyone how disappointed he was in his oldest son.

"On the other hand, Will's mother was always physically present. However, she was perpetually pregnant and busy caring for the ever-growing family. She also lost five children which would have taken a huge emotional toll. By all reports she was not well and was weak most of the time. Quite likely she did not have the energy to sufficiently nurture her first born. He was on his own.

"So what happens to people like Will as they become adults? In general, they all seem to use the same play-book. They strive to be perfect in an effort to please their parents; it's hard to be perfect. They over-achieve as they attempt to live up to expectations. Even this is often not enough.

"They ultimately develop behaviors in an effort to secure the approval and love they never received when they were young. They work harder than everyone else, perform endless acts of kindness and become extremely generous in the subconscious hope that people will notice. As a result, they are told over and over how amazing and wonderful they are. This feeds that unmet childhood need.

"They also try to fill that empty personal place by engaging in things that make them feel good, even if it's temporary. Things like buying yachts, bigger yachts, mansions, second homes, third homes, Pullman cars, Pierce Arrow automobiles, plastic surgery, companies and more companies. The list is endless. They try to stimulate the feel good part of their brain with food, nicotine, gambling, poker and stock-market speculation.

"Does any of this sound familiar, Gus? Don't you think this is a reasonably fair description of the behavior that William Boyce Thompson exhibited? Perhaps counseling at a young age could have saved him from the ever-faster treadmill he'd created in an effort to feel loved and needed. However, back in the 1800s and early 1900s, nobody talked about these issues and there were no experts. Heck, we barely talk about them now.

"There really is no one to blame. Thompson and his parents were products of the times in which they lived. All I know is I am sad for him.

"Concerning the stroke, aside from the obvious paralysis, he likely had impaired swallowing ability too, which caused silent aspiration. This would explain the hoarseness and almost inaudible quality of his voice; it is quite possible he developed aspiration pneumonia that led to his ultimate death. The Colonel would have benefitted from modern day swallow studies, speech pathologists and a modified diet. However, these approaches were yet invented.

"He had a brilliant, inquisitive and innovative mind and he had a kind heart; I wish he were still around so I could help him and call him my friend."

"Bobbi, thanks for helping me understand more about life, at least human life. I've come to the conclusion that it's a lot simpler being a cactus. I just stand in one place on Magma Ridge, day after day, and listen to the gossip and the tour leaders.

"Would you mind doing something else for me, Bobbi? I am curious about what happened to Alder Manor, the yacht, the Pierce Arrow, the fancy Pullman car and the Institute for Plant Research in Yonkers. I'd like to find out what became of his wife, his daughter and the grandchildren. Gertrude never returned to the Arboretum after his death; there never was any final conversation.

"I have no friends out east who can supply me with information and the tour guides don't talk about these topics. I think I speak for all the furred, feathered and thorny individuals that live here when I say we loved the Colonel and we have continued to grieve; there never was any opportunity for us to ask questions or for closure."

"Gus, that sounds like an excellent idea. I need something to take my mind off the rather tragic way in which the Colonel died. See, I've already stopped crying. I'll start by discussing Alder Manor, but I expect that when I'm done, you'll fill me in on the more recent history that transpired here at the arboretum too. Is that a deal?"

"Yes, it's a deal," Gus said.

"After Thompson died, Gertrude was provided with twenty million dollars as long as she resided at the Manor. I can't begin to imagine the costs involved in maintaining seventy-two rooms, twenty-five bedrooms and twenty-two acres of manicured gardens. Many other mansions along the Hudson were abandoned or demolished during this time, but not the Manor.

"Gertrude resided at Alder Manor until she died on August 27, 1950. She never did remarry. For whatever reason, she willed the Manor to the Roman Catholic Diocese of New York; given the Colonel's well known antipathy toward organized religions, I can imagine he rolled over in his grave several times at Sleepy Hollow cemetery when he heard about this gift. However, he would have been delighted to know the mansion was going to be used as an all-girls school. It was repurposed and became the Mary Elizabeth Seton High School.

"In 1960, the Manor morphed into the Elizabeth Seton Junior College; ultimately Iona College became involved in a merger in 1989. During this period, the Manor was placed on the National Registry of Historic Places. Unfortunately taxes, maintenance and repairs became cost-prohibitive and the mansion was locked and abandoned in 1995.

"Over time, the property was parceled off and the city bought an outer building that became an elementary school. The rest of the buildings were vandalized; fixtures were removed; items were looted and as a final insult, graffiti was left behind.

"After years of fundraising, an Irish-American organization called Tara Circle purchased the old Manor and began a cleaning and restoration project. They used the building for concerts, weddings and also conducted classes in Irish music and dance.

"Alder Manor was also used as a movie set for the filming of The Royal *Tenenbaums* starring Owen Wilson, Gene Hackman, Gwyneth Paltrow, Bill Murray, Ben Stiller, Alec Baldwin and others.

"*Mona Lisa's Smile,* featuring Julia Roberts, and *A Beautiful Mind* with Jennifer Connelly and Russell Crowe were also filmed there. More recently the Lela Goren Group has assumed ownership and is attempting to reintroduce the Manor as an arts and special event venue."

"That's really interesting, Bobbi. I wish I could see those movies. Perhaps you could bring your lap top up here one evening and we could watch them together.

"Now tell me about the Thompsons's daughter, Margaret. What in the world happened to her?"

"Margaret, who was called Peggy throughout her life, was born in 1897 and she had an especially good relationship with the Colonel. She married Ted Schulze II in 1916 and they had two children: Ted Schulze III, who was born in 1920 and Margaret, who was also called Peggy, born in 1921.

"In 1930, and just two months before Thompson's death, Margaret was installed as a director of the Boyce Thompson Arboretum. Gus, when I discovered this fact during my research, I felt incredibly happy. I think the Colonel would have been so proud to have his daughter take an interest in his grand project.

"The Schulze marriage ended in divorce and Margaret went on to meet Anthony Joseph Drexel

Biddle. He was from a wealthy Philadelphia family, a champion amateur boxer and a war veteran; he was also the American Ambassador to Poland. They were married in 1931 and had a baby boy early in their new marriage: he died at birth. I'm sure this was a period of great stress for the Schulze children who were in grade school at the time. They had to deal with the break-up of the original family, cope with a new step-father, move to Europe and adjust to being far from their father and grandparents.

Margaret and Anthony Biddle
(Courtesy of Boyce Thompson)

"Margaret became a celebrated collector of antiquities, silver and Vermeil flatware. In fact, much of her collection was donated to the White House during the Eisenhower presidency and is now used and displayed in the Vermeil Room.

"This marriage also ended in divorce and unfortunately Margaret passed away in 1956 at the relatively young age of 58. You won't believe this, Gus. The cause of her death was neurological: a stroke caused by a brain hemorrhage. There was clearly a pattern going on in the Thompson family.

"Her son, Ted, was around thirty-six years of age when his mother died and a short time later, he took her place as a director on the Board. As a kid, he had never visited the arboretum, much to the chagrin of his grandfather. However, he quickly made up for lost time and became president. He personally donated a portion of his Magma Copper stocks to the arboretum and specified they were to fund a scholarship for a deserving undergraduate botany student who wanted to pursue a Master's degree. The money would also pay for the construction of a small greenhouse for the recipient's use.

"The lucky first winner was Ian Price from Wye College in London, England. He spent his first year of study at the University of Arizona and then moved to Superior to be near the arboretum, where he completed his groundbreaking research on the propagation of eucalyptus from cuttings. He defended his thesis and was awarded a Master's degree in 1961. This was a joyful moment for everyone, especially Ted Schulze, and he made plans to create more scholarships. Unfortunately he died suddenly and unexpectedly in December of 1962, while visiting France. He was only forty-two years of age.

"His sister, Peggy Schulze, never visited the arboretum as a kid either. However, she frequently saw her Thompson grandparents when they were home in Yonkers. Apparently she had a great relationship with Grandpa Thompson until he passed in 1930. She was nine years old at the time and then she was off to Poland.

"During her teenage years, Peggy lived the life of an ambassador's stepdaughter. She attended social events frequented by the rich and famous and returned the flirtations of the Polish Prince Alexander of Hohenlohe-Wadenburg-Schillingsfurst. They married in 1939 as World War II was just getting started. He initially served in the military and after several harrowing experiences, the couple escaped from Poland. They eventually moved to the United States where he found work in the

Polish Embassy in Washington D.C. They had two children, Catherine and Christian.

"Their marriage struggled and after 10 years they finally separated; the Prince did not deal with the situation well and shot himself in his left chest. Peggy rejoined him while he miraculously recovered and then she left for good and filed for divorce. I have no idea what happened to the Prince or how often his two children would see their father in the future.

"A year later she became the second wife of the well-known American singer, Morton Downey. He had five children from his first marriage to the actress Barbara Bennett. He was a devout Catholic and demanded that Peggy's first marriage be annulled before he would marry her. Apparently he was successful in personally pursuing this goal; I wonder if he had his first marriage annulled as well.

"Given there were seven children between them, it would have been a busy household. One of the kids, Morton Downey Jr., went on to become a famous, very confrontational, American talk-show host.

"Peggy died in 1964 at about the same age as her brother, Ted. She succumbed to complications related to breast cancer surgery."

"Bobbi, all of this information about celebrity, lavish lifestyles, divorce and early deaths has been really riveting. On the other hand, it has left me feeling sad. Do you have a similar feeling?"

"I think the issue that caught my attention the most, Gus, was the effect all the adult decisions must have had on the children. I've already mentioned the Schulze kids, Ted and Peggy, and the stress they must have experienced. Let's not forget the Hohenlohe children, Catherine and Christian. They were not even ten years old when their parents broke up and their father shot himself and almost died; then before they knew it, they had four Downey step-brothers and a step-sister. Talk about upsetting the pecking order. They also had to contend with the death of their mother from breast cancer when they were barely into their twenties.

"Christian Hohenlohe eventually became a member of the Boyce Thompson Arboretum Board of Directors too, continuing the tradition that had started with the Colonel's daughter, of always having a Thompson descendant on the board. Christian rose to the position of vice president and later his son, Paul, followed in his footsteps. Can you imagine how pleased the Colonel would have been?

"To answer your question Gus, I am feeling sad as well. There is an old saying that money or social status can't buy you happiness. It is a rather simple idea and I think it may have been applicable to the lives we have just visited. Of course many of these individuals are not around anymore to provide us with their version of the story; I'm not sure they would want to anyway. Some people seek privacy when it comes to personal matters. Others in similar situations write memoirs in an effort to clarify and teach. Perhaps there is no reason for us to feel sad: they may well have been perfectly happy and fulfilled individuals. In the end, we all find our way forward and there should be no place for judgment or criticism."

"Bobbi, I really appreciate your perspective here. Now I'm going to push my luck and ask if you could talk about two more topics; then I promise I'll take over and talk about the arboretum. I am curious about what happened to the enormous yacht? And whatever happened to the Boyce Thompson Institute for Plant Research?"

"All right, Gus, because you asked so nicely, I'll begin with the yacht named Alder.

The yacht named Alder

(Courtesy of Boyce Thompson)

"As you can see, she was enormous at 294 feet. I have no idea whether Mrs. Thompson ever used the yacht again. Did she dismiss the crew? Did she rent the yacht to other individuals? Was maintenance performed? Or did the *Alder* simply stay docked where the Colonel last docked her in Miami? There are so many unanswered questions.

"In any event, she donated the vessel to the US Navy in 1939; I assume Gertrude received tax advice from her accountants and lawyers. During the next year, *Alder* was converted to a war ship and renamed *Jamestown PG-55*. She was initially used for training. However, as the Second World War ramped up and the Japanese became involved, the ship was repurposed and fitted with guns. The Jamestown was then directed to the South Pacific where she escorted convoys and pulled barges loaded with supplies, bombs and fuel.

Photo No. 19-N-32984 USS Jamestown (PG-55) on 23 July 1942

USS Jamestown

(Courtesy of Boyce Thompson)

"She also became involved in servicing PT boats and at one point was credited with a hit on an enemy submarine.

"The *Jamestown* received a much-needed overhaul in 1944 and was put back in service until 1946. The crew and the ship received a Presidential Unit Citation and she was finally decommissioned.

"The one-time palatial yacht was finally sold into private hands and commenced a commercial career; she was renamed the *Marosana*. In 1961, while hauling bananas from Ecuador to Tampa, Florida, she sprung a leak, floundered and sank several hundred miles west of Panama. It was a rather inglorious end for an incredible ship.

"You also requested an update on the Boyce Thompson Institute for Plant Research. Let me refresh your memory. After the Colonel returned from witnessing Russian starvation, he established the Institute and charged it with the task of better understanding plants in order to enhance world food supply. He also expected discoveries in conservation, environmental protection and improvements in human health.

"Because this was something he was passionate about, he wanted the operation nearby where he could exercise large measures of personal control. He purchased land across the street from Alder Manor and constructed the Institute.

"Thompson hired as his first director, Mr. William Crocker, head of the Department of Plant Physiology at the University of Chicago. Crocker assembled an incredible team of experts that included a proto-zoologist, an entomologist, a plant physiologist and a plant pathologist: there were twelve scientists in all. The Institute featured state-of-the-art labs, microscopes and hothouses and it was up and researching by 1920.

"In spite of Thompson's death and with the help of a $10 million endowment, programs continued until the 1970s, when it became cost prohibitive to operate in Yonkers; urban pollution was also contaminating the research.

"The state of New York in conjunction with Cornell University stepped in and the Institute was relocated to Cornell, where it remains today. The remaining structures in Yonkers were the subject of decay and vandalism. Ultimately they were owned by the city and sold to a developer in 2015. I am happy to report that a commercial initiative called the Boyce Thompson Center was opened in 2017. It features restaurants, medical offices, and space for other retail operations. There are numerous signs paying tribute to the vision of William Boyce Thompson.

"Concerning the Institute at Cornell, there has been great success to boast about through the years. The herbicide, 2,4-D was discovered; major breakthroughs in tomato genetics, edible vaccines, inhaled insulin, rust fungus protection, pine beetle control and ozone preservation are only a few of the accomplishments attributable to the Institute.

"As of 2017, this internationally acclaimed facility featured fifteen faculty run labs and employed 110 researchers from over forty countries. Their mission now includes improving food crops, demystifying human and plant immune systems, and revealing alternative sources of renewable energy. To be honest Gus, I don't think the Colonel had any idea what he had set in motion here; I think he would be flabbergasted.

"Okay, it's your turn now. I'd like to know what happened to Picket Post House, the arboretum, Nat Patterson, Doby Tom, the Pullman and Pierce Arrow cars and everything else. I'm all ears."

"You're a tough act to follow, Bobbi. I think because all your questions are connected to the garden, I'll talk about the arboretum and you'll obtain the complete picture.

"To say the least, the Colonel's death in 1930 was a huge blow. The stock market crash and subsequent Great Depression undermined the amount of funding that Thompson had calculated to maintain his arboretum; the project would be dogged by financial concerns that continue to this day. To make matters worse, Crider decided to resign as director in 1934: he had led the development of the arboretum for ten years.

"He went to work for the US Department of Agriculture and organized their soil conservation program. Remember, this was the time of the Dust Bowl and under Crider's leadership, soil conservation nurseries were constructed where stabilizing plants were grown and distributed throughout the affected areas.

"Back at the arboretum, Gibson ably took over as Director. Most of the ground crew stayed, including Nat. However, soon after the Colonel died, Doby Tom retired and was surprised to learn a monthly pension had been written into Thompson's will, just for him. The Colonel's generosity appeared to be limitless.

"Picket Post House sat empty because Mrs. Thompson never returned to the Arboretum. The Pullman car never graced the siding again and the Pierce Arrow was sold. I have tried to track down the car and whether it is still in existence; I've had no luck. The Pierce would be worth a small fortune by now.

"The gardens grew and matured. Fountains and picnic areas were created and the public cherished the place. However, financial concerns continued to weigh heavily and in 1946, a decision was made to sell Picket Post House: the proceeds were badly needed.

"The new owners were Walter and Ida Franklin. They converted the home into a bed and breakfast and their most famous customer was the wife and two daughters of the celebrated polar explorer, Admiral Byrd. After two years as owners, they sold the venture to William and Mabel Steinegger. Their most famous client was Jack Dempsey, the former heavyweight boxing champion of the world; he stopped by for lunch.

"During their ownership, the Colonel's bedroom house burned down in 1960 due to an electrical fire. It was not rebuilt and the charred remains were removed. The Steineggers sold the home to the Roses in 1963 and I'll tell you more about them later.

"Back at the arboretum, Nat Patterson continued to work his magic with irrigation and he and Gibson established an incredible working relationship. Under Gibson's direction, Nat rebuilt the garage at the north house, created parking lots, built more trails and constantly removed fallen tree limbs. He was a tireless employee and perhaps missed two days of work in a forty year career.

"He was also a grandfather many times over. His son, Morgan, had grown up and married; Morgan had eight kids who had the run of the gardens. They all continued to live in the Indian Village and I watched from my spot above the main trail as the children played tricks on the arboretum visitors. Their favorite ruse was to gather as a group and stop and stare in unison… at nothing. Visitors would stop and join them and would strain to see what was so interesting. Then the kids would start laughing and run off; I would crack up laughing too.

“Nat was unhurried and confident in his work. There appeared to be no rush to get things done before his time on earth was over. He was often heard to say that a person continues to live, even after death, and there is lots of time to complete unfinished projects in that spiritual future. Nat lived a primitive life in his hut, year after year; he did not crave luxuries.

“Patterson saw directors, curators and many ground crew workers come and go. He served longer than any other employee at the Arboretum. In 1965, he was excited to hear that the University of Arizona was going to partner with the Boyce Thompson Arboretum. Like everyone else, he hoped that research would once again flourish with a new funding source in place.

“When the university assumed management, Nat had just turned eighty and he was let go from his job. Given his age, the dismissal was not really that unexpected. Nat assumed he would continue to live in his hut at the Indian Village. However, he was told he had to leave the arboretum and he protested, arguing that the Colonel had given him a deed to the land on which his meager little shelter sat. He was not able to produce the title because it had been destroyed in a small fire years before; a copy could not be found in the archives either.

"As a result, Nat had to leave his home of forty years next to Picket Post and find a new way forward. Management moved swiftly to bulldoze all the Indian Village huts into oblivion, including Nat's. All the rubble was quickly removed in what appeared to be an effort to leave no trace. It appears that Nat harbored no animosity; even in retirement, he volunteered almost daily, watering his favorite plants and picking up litter.

"He died on April 25, 1968: four months shy of his eighty-third birthday. His was a life well lived."

"Gus, you've done it again with this story about Nat. You have moved me to tears and I'm fumbling for some tissue paper. I'm angry too. Management at the time seems to have acted in a very heavy-handed and shameful manner concerning this long-standing employee and friend of the Colonel."

"We all felt that way, Bobbi, and my plant and animal friends talked about organizing protests. In the end, we decided to follow Nat's example and carry on with grace and dignity. There was no place in his life for bitterness or anger and we decided not to be governed by retaliation either.

After all, we had an arboretum to participate in and a Colonel to honor.

"There have been a dizzying number of programs, directors, curators, government initiative workers, professors, students, grounds crew, maintenance staff and volunteers throughout the years. Storms have come and gone; bridges have been built, only to be washed out. Snowfalls and ice storms have brought down branches; the university has researched cork-oak trees and jojoba; the place has always been a beehive of activity.

"Then, in 1976, the Arizona State Parks joined the existing partners and a tripartite agreement of oversight was put into place. Not only was some new money added to the equation, there were new ideas too: a formal volunteer program was started; endangered Desert Pupfish and Gila Top Minnow were introduced to Ayer Lake, sans alligator of course! The Arboretum was placed on the National Historic Registry and a new Visitor Center was built, as well as the children's garden, the Australian drover shack and pavilion and the excellent demonstration garden where the public could learn about xeriscaping. The construction of the suspension bridge made the high trail accessible and participation in the Desert Legume Project (DELEP) became of paramount importance.

"There have been some failures too: the Director's bridge; a second well and plans to create a new Garden of Eden by relocating plants from the original gardens in Turkmenistan. As a reminder, Thompson did not hit a home run with every mine he invested in either. If we learned anything from him, it was that you have to be inquisitive, think big and sometimes take a calculated risk. You will never fail if you aren't willing to try something new.

"Of course there were generous donors like the Taylors, the Wings, Rodica Heinz and the Wallaces that made possible the legume, herb and pollinator gardens, the children's area and the brand new cactus exhibit. Bobbi, I can't begin to mention everything and everybody. However, I think I've given you a brief overview of what has become of the Colonel's garden."

"You've done just fine, Gus. Remember the point of my book was to cover the early years of the arboretum and now, in a very succinct way, you've tied a bow on the whole story. There will be more formal histories written that will provide a complete accounting. However, they won't be featuring you and for that I am sorry. Is there anything else you'd like to say?"

"Oh my goodness, I almost forgot to tell you! The most exciting thing of all occurred in 2008 when we had an old family member return to the arboretum. I'm talking about the Picket Post House. She was purchased by the State Parks from the Rose family for 2.9 million dollars and she was even more famous now because of her starring role in the 1997 movie called *U-Turn*. It featured Jennifer Lopez, Sean Penn and Nick Nolte and a great fight scene took place in the living room where the Colonel once thumped around with his cane!

The main living room, where the Colonel thumped and Nick Nolte got whacked. (Courtesy of Marriane Jenson)

"Picket Post needs a lot of work, but at least she's home. I don't think I've left anything of significance out, Bobbi. Before you leave, could you give me some water and make sure you return to show me your book once it's published."

Gus and me

EPILOGUE

My manuscript was finished and the first proof from the publishing company arrived in the mail. I had to share it with Gus and drove to the arboretum late in the day. He was exactly where I'd last seen him and he hadn't changed a bit. I walked along my well-worn path to his brown feet, looked up and showed him the book. He loved the title and especially his photo. He said, "Bobbi, I think this is the best picture of me ever. I usually have my eyes closed or I've got a thorn or two out of place."

I held the book over my head and leafed through the pages. Gus can't read and I promised to come back with the final rendition and read it to him, cover to cover.

Gus told me he watches as I conduct general tours every Sunday morning. He smiles when I wave to him each time I pass by. However, he doesn't want to say anything and disrupt my train of thought.

The book project had allowed us to become great friends and I wanted to give him a present to thank him for all the time he had spent telling his story. I thought long and hard about the kind of things a saguaro cactus could use and nothing came to mind. I even searched the internet looking for gifts for the saguaro in your life and there were no suggestions. I was coming up completely blank, and then it came to me; now was the time to tell him about it.

"Gus, I have a present for you. It is my way of saying thanks for helping make this book special."

He protested, saying a gift was unnecessary. I persisted and told him he must accept it because I was about to break all kinds of rules to secure the present. Now I had piqued his curiosity and he perked up and leaned forward ever so slightly.

"What is it, Bobbi?"

"Gus, my gift to you will take place next spring after your flowers have bloomed; after you've gone batty and your fruit has ripened. I'm going to collect some of your seeds and plant them under several nearby nurse trees. I will keep them safe and well-watered. Gus, I am going to surround you with a family. Tell me, what do you think about this plan?"

Gus stood there; he was speechless and then the tears flowed from everywhere. He glistened as the setting sun danced on his rugged features and all he could say, in an almost inaudible whisper was, "I love you Bobbi."

There was nothing more to say.

Bobbi Lancaster, 2017
(Photo by Joanne West)

AUTHOR COMMENT

Hello everyone. My name is Dr. Bobbi Lancaster and I am a family physician, retired professional golfer, spouse, parent, speaker and civil rights advocate. My wife is a nurse practitioner and an American Kennel Club Breeder of Merit. She raises Havanese puppies and I am the official poop scooper. And Gus and I really are good friends.

During the summer of 2018, I was recovering from a major professional setback. I sought a healing and quiet place and was drawn to Boyce Thompson Arboretum. How many of you have gravitated there for the same reason? It is about thirty minutes from my Gold Canyon home and the walking paths and scenery are pitch-perfect. After several visits I found myself yearning for more information about the place.

I stopped at the visitor center and was disappointed to find there was not a single book written about the arboretum. After I visited several more times and attended specialty tours, I made the following promises to myself.

First, I was going to become a general tour guide and educate the public about this magical place.

Second, I was going to write a book for guests to enjoy long after their visit. However, I wanted the book to be unique and appeal to young and old alike. That's when I concocted the idea of having Gus, a saguaro cactus, serve as the narrator.

I hope you enjoy this book. You will be sadly mistaken if you think it is just for kids. The history, science and insights I offer are based upon everything I've learned over the course of a lifetime. The people, plants and animals featured are more than just names and dates. Once upon a time they were all very much alive and I have attempted to bring them back to life so you can really get to know and understand them.

By the way, I am donating every single dollar this book generates to the arboretum. To be blunt, it is struggling financially and every penny helps. We all know the special spot in our heart this beautiful garden occupies and I think we have a shared responsibility to keep places like this preserved for generations to come.

In closing, you will learn that Gus was once able to talk with an Apache woman called Two Spirit. I want to share with you that I am a transgender individual and if I were Native American, I would be called a Two Spirit as well. In that culture, people like me are respected because we have experienced life in both genders. There is an assumption that this confers wisdom upon us. You can be the judge of that.

If you look closely, you can find Gus standing on Magma Ridge. When I am long gone someday, I hope you will continue to wave to him and his kids for me.

From your friend in nature,
Bobbi

ACKNOWLEDGEMENTS

There are countless people to thank who assisted me during the writing of this book. I am not going to attempt to list all of them because I will accidently leave someone out and feelings will be unintentionally hurt. However, there are several individuals that I must acknowledge.

Sylvia Lee is a long-time volunteer at the arboretum and serves as the historian. She has been researching and collecting stories and photos of the park for years and will be publishing the definitive history book in the future. We first met when I attended her lecture about William Boyce Thompson and I was impressed with her command of the facts. She patiently answered my never-ending questions and graciously shared her research. Sylvia guided me to secret historical places and I became even more enchanted with the arboretum. She mentored me during my training as a general tour guide and enthusiastically supported the writing of this book. We placed our friendship at risk when I allowed her to read and critique the early drafts. I would never have written Putting Down Roots if I hadn't met Sylvia and Gus would have remained forever silent on Magma Ridge.

Anthea Penne is an award winning Canadian author (*Old Stones* and *Reckoning)* who I met by chance almost thirteen years ago when she was vacationing in Gold Canyon. Lucy and I bumped into Anthea and her mother when they were out for a walk in our neighborhood and a friendship took root. I was a fledgling writer at the time and she has served as my editor ever since. Anthea always makes time for me, even though she is very busy writing, editing and teaching students. She has her work cut out dealing with me: tightening prose, correcting grammar, adding and subtracting punctuation. She is unflinchingly supportive and believes in the importance of my storytelling and messaging. Anthea is helping me find my voice.

Lacey Pacheco is the Director of Education and the Librarian at Boyce Thompson Arboretum. Presently she is wearing even more hats because of the recent retirement of several staff members. However she has always enthusiastically set aside time to honor my multiple requests for access to archival photos and documents. Her trust in my mission and her support made all the difference. Lacey has a plan to ensure all the proceeds from the sale of this book flow to the correct department.

Rick Wright certainly warrants honorable mention too. I met him in the summer of 2018 when he visited the arboretum as an honored guest and conducted bird walks and an unusual bird sitting. As a brand new volunteer, I had the pleasure of introducing him each day and this required studying his biography. His accomplishments boggle the mind. He has lead bird and art tours for Victor Emanuel Nature Tours around the world, authored multiple birding field guides and has lectured extensively. He is also an editor, has a PhD in German and has worked as a professor of medieval studies. I thought Rick would be the perfect person to review my book and write the foreword. During a rather bold moment, I connected with him and Rick readily agreed to accept the challenge. His narrative at the start of this book is something I'll always treasure.

Dr. Steven Semken and I have met only once; I attended a geology lecture he presented at the arboretum. He patiently answered all my questions. In spite of barely knowing me, he readily agreed to read my book and critique the geology concepts I present in chapter two. I will be forever grateful for his comments and the time he took out of his busy work schedule at Arizona State University.

I would be remiss if I did not thank Boyce Thompson. He is the grand-nephew of William Boyce Thompson and an accomplished author in his own right. We have never met, but I read his stories about the Thompson family and connected with him through email. He graciously allowed me to use some of the photos he owns because he understood the proceeds of the book were being given to the arboretum. I also have to thank Marianne Jenson, a professional photographer in Arizona, for the use of her beautiful photo of the Picket Post great room.

Finally, I must acknowledge my wife and best buddy, Lucy. I am not very adept yet with many important writing skills: the advanced use of a computer, spell check, Microsoft Word, scanning, Adobe photo shop and typing. She is bombarded constantly with grammatical questions and exhibits the patience of Job. Lucy is delighted when I leave to see patients or play golf because it allows her to luxuriate for a few hours in well-deserved silence.

CPSIA information can be obtained
at www.ICGtesting.com
Printed in the USA
FSHW020736210319

9 780578 452463